Leading Ladies

A COMEDY

by Ken Ludwig

A SAMUEL FRENCH ACTING EDITION

SAMUEL FRENCH

FOUNDED 1830

New York Hollywood London Toronto

SAMUELFRENCH.COM

IMPORTANT BILLING AND CREDIT REQUIREMENTS

All producers of **LEADING LADIES** must give credit to the Author of the Play in all programs distributed in connection with performances of the Play, and in all instances in which the title of the Play appears for the purposes of advertising, publicizing or otherwise exploiting the Play and /or a production. The name of the Author must appear on a separate line on which no other name appears, immediately following the title and must appear in size of type not less than fifty percent of the size of the title type.

In addition the following billing must be in the same size, typeface and boldness as that afforded the licensee producer in its presentation credit above the title.

Originally produced
by

The Cleveland Play House   and   Alley Theatre
Michael Bloom, Artistic Director   Gregory Boyd, Artistic Director
Dean Gladden, Managing Director   Terry Dwyer , Managing Director
on September 7th, 2004   on October 15th, 2004

LEADING LADIES had its world premiere at the Alley Theatre, Gregory Boyd, Artistic Director, in association with the Cleveland Playhouse, Michael Bloom, Artistic Director, Dean R.Gladden, Managing Director, on October 15th, 2004. The Scenic Designer was Neil Patel, the Costume Designer was Judith Dolan, the Lighting Designer was David Weiner and the Sound Designer was John Gromada and Associate Sound Designer was Ryan Rumery. The Choreographer was Michael Tapley, the Stage Manager was Terry Cranshaw and the Assistant Stage Manager was Amy Liljegren. The production was under the direction of Ken Ludwig with the following cast:

MEG	Erin Dilly
LEO	Brent Barrett
JACK	Christopher Duva
AUDREY	Lacey Kohl
DUNCAN	Mark Jacoby
FLORENCE	Jane Connell
DOC	Dan Lauria
BUTCH	Tim McGeever

CHARACTERS

Meg
Leo
Jack
Audrey
Duncan
Florence
Doc
Butch

SETTING

The play, essentially, has one set, and the majority of the action takes place in the large, handsome living room of the biggest house in York, Pennsylvania in 1958. The room has large French doors up right leading out to a garden. We can see the patio and shrubbery through the glass. Double doors down left lead to the vestibule, a hall and the front door. Double doors down right lead to the kitchen and additional rooms. There is a grand staircase that leads, at the top, to a bedroom door and a landing which leads off left. Under the staircase, up center, is an open doorway that leads to additional rooms. As we'll find out, all of these rooms are interconnected off stage. It's a grand house with a second staircase that we can't see.

Scene two of the first act is set in the Shrewsbury, Pa. Moose Lodge - an area of stage in front of a curtain.

Scene three of the first act is set inside a train, and all we see are two seats and an aisle.

This play is dedicated to my mother, Louise Ludwig, who was the kindest person I have ever known. And the most fun.

ACT I

Scene 1

(The handsome, spacious living room of a beautiful, well-appointed house in York, Pennsylvania in the spring of 1958. York is a quiet town in an area of gently rolling hills in southern Pennsylvania known as the Amish country. York was once, briefly, the capital of the Unites States, during the American Revolution, when the Articles of Confederation were kept here after Congress left Philadelphia under threat of invasion. So it's old country, proud country, settled by the English and the Germans, the latter bringing with them a plain-spoken, plain-dressed brand of religion that has been here ever since. The food here is rich and deep, the farmland outside town is magnificent and the people here have a great tradition of music. The point of all this is that York is filled with good, wise people, many of whom are happy to be just where they are — but some of whom would love to see the world just over the horizon. As the lights come up, MEG SNIDER, dressed to go out for the evening, ENTERS at the top of the stairs. She looks around and sees no one below; then she hurries down the stairs to the French doors that open out to the garden. As she makes the turn at the bottom corner of the banister, she swoops around in a grand arc, full of joy and anticipation. Our play is all about MEG, really, so we should take a very good look at her while we have the chance. She is a

local girl in her early 30s. She's vivacious, with enormous warmth and a great sense of humor. She also has the fresh, unstudied beauty that most women would kill for. MEG, however, is that second kind of Yorker. She knows there's a big world outside York, Pa., but she hasn't seen much of it yet. She harbors a world of dreams, and sleeps on them every night. They keep her alive, but she doesn't know it.)

MEG. Duncan? ... Duncan?!

DUNCAN. *(Off.)* Coming!

MEG. Oh, Duncan, please hurry up! It's 5:30! And it takes at least 45 minutes to get to Shrewsbury. And the show starts at seven!

(DUNCAN WOOLEY ENTERS, fixing his clerical collar. He's the local minister and substantially older than MEG. He's a good man at heart, but rather fussy, set in his ways, a bit scatterbrained, and lives in his own world.)

DUNCAN. Meg, I'm moving as fast as I can. I normally don't go out in the evenings. You know that. I can't get organized. I-I can't find things...

MEG. I'm sorry, Duncan, but —

DUNCAN. I hope you're not going to rush me after we get married.

MEG. Of course not, but I —

DUNCAN. It's not as if I don't want to get married. But I don't like rushing. It's almost... un-Christian the way you do it.

MEG. Is it? I'm sorry.

DUNCAN. Kiss kiss?

MEG. Kiss kiss. *(They kiss lightly.)* But Duncan, we can't be late for this!

DUNCAN. If you want the truth, I don't particularly want to go anyway.

MEG. How can you say that?! It's Shakespeare! "Scenes from Shakespeare!" How often do we get a chance like this, living in York, Pennsylvania?

DUNCAN. Not very often, thank the Lord.

MEG. Duncan!

DUNCAN. Who's in this again?

MEG. It stars these two really wonderful actors from England. Leo Clark and Jack Gable. I saw them do a show like this in Philadelphia about two years ago. Don't you remember? I told you about it.

DUNCAN. Did you?

MEG. Oh, they were so wonderful! And to hear that language just... rolling over you in wave after wave. Oh. I think I love the theatre more than anything in the whole world.

DUNCAN. Nonsense.

MEG. I do!

DUNCAN. Meg. Theatre can be wonderful of course. At times. When it's something like the York County Bell-Ringers Annual Easter Pageant. Or The Messiah when they bring real sheep on stage. But there's something rather... troubling about professional theatre. The people in it are so... theatrical.

MEG. Duncan —

DUNCAN. So loose and flamboyant.

MEG. That's not how I —

DUNCAN. Now take these actors of yours. What are they called again?

MEG. Clark and Gable.

DUNCAN. Right.

MEG. They're fantastic.

DUNCAN. Meg, they're playing at the Shrewsbury Moose Lodge. They can't be that "fantastic."

MEG. Well they must have had an open date on their touring schedule, but —

DUNCAN. You know, the church has never looked very kindly upon play-going as a phenomenon, as a way of —

MEG. Duncan, please! Can we go now?! It's late! And you promised!

DUNCAN. All right, all right! I'll start the car.

(He starts to EXIT, then walks right back to MEG.)

DUNCAN. Problem.

MEG. What?

DUNCAN. Big problem.

MEG. What is it?

DUNCAN. We don't have a car.

MEG. What do you mean?

DUNCAN. *(Defensively.)* Well, I drove straight here from visiting some of my congregants, who are ill, and as I was getting out of the car, Mr. Morton walked by and told me that his car had broken down and he needed to buy groceries for his family — and take his wife to see her mother — and I said use my car, as long as you bring it back at the proper time.

MEG. So?

DUNCAN. I told him I didn't need it till eight. I just remembered.

MEG. Oh, Duncan!

DUNCAN, I'm sorry, my dear. It slipped my mind.

MEG. How could you do this?!

DUNCAN. I'm very sorry.

MEG. Now we'll miss it! I can't believe it! Oh damn!

DUNCAN. *(Scandalized.)* Meg!

MEG. Well I'm upset! I wanted to see Leo Clark!

DUNCAN. An actor.

MEG. Yes! Exactly!

DUNCAN. Now, now, we can still have fun. We can meet up with old friends and have dinner and chat. Ooh this could be good. I'll call the Kunkles. See if they're busy.

(He starts dialing.)

MEG. Duncan, the Kunkles are a hundred years old!

DUNCAN. Only Grandma Kunkle. And when she's awake, she's a riot. HELLO?! IS THAT GRANDMA KUNKLE?!!

MEG. Oh, Duncan ...

(MEG sighs with frustration and collapses on the sofa.)

Scene 2

(We hear a recording of a popular, upbeat song of the period and a raucous crowd having a good time. We're in an auditorium in Shrewsbury, Pennsylvania, that night. DOCTOR MYERS comes down the aisle, shaking hands with his friends and slapping their backs. He's the Chief Moose – a crusty, likeable curmudgeon, a country doctor who takes no guff from anybody. He wears the distinctive red fez of the Moose. He bounds onto the stage and starts the meeting.)

DOC MYERS. Ladies and Gentlemen... Ladies and Gentlemen! Thank you and welcome to the June, 1952 general meeting of the Loyal Order of the Moose, Shrewsbury Pennsylvania Lodge Number 84! Awhoo!!

*("Awhoo" is the Sound of the Moose. When DOC MYERS does the
call, the other Moose in the lodge call back to him.)*

DOC MYERS. We hope you're having a heck of a good time
tonight, and that you're all looking forward to the very special buffet spread we have waiting for you tonight across the hall — pre-
pared exclusively by Pyemyers Pastries and Pigtrotters. Their motto
is: "We go the whole hog and use the whole hog." Thank you, Carl
Pyemyer and family. Now tonight I have the honor of presenting
what you might call a "departure" from our usual monthly entertainment. In April we gave you "Hee Haw Hocum," a night of fero-
cious fiddling and hillbilly hilarity that as you'll remember raised
the roof and brought the house down. Then in May, we saw the one
and only "Mister Presto," whose amazing feats of prestidigatorial
perfection brought us standing to our feet. *(Personally, I will never
forget how he manipulated his eggs and made that sausage of his
appear out of nowhere.)* Well folks, tonight we're plowing some
new ground and bringing you some very special entertainment, en-
titled, believe it or not, "Scenes from Shakespeare" starring two actors who hail from London, England, coming to us direct from their
last engagement at the Elks of Scranton, please give a Moose Lodge
welcome to Leo Clark and Jack Gable! Awhoo!!

*(Awhoo!! As DOC EXITS, the curtain flies, the lights change — and
we're on a battlefield in England in the 1400s. Trumpets sound!
Banners wave! We hear the sounds of war and we see a flimsy
castle in the distance! These effects, unfortunately, are a bit
down-at-heel. This is, after all, a tour of one-nighters, not the
RSC. So the banners are a bit ragged, the music a bit tinny, and
the one piece of scenery, the castle, can be folded for traveling.)*

LEADING LADIES

(HENRY THE FIFTH, played by LEO CLARK, rushes on in full
battle gear, waving his sword and rallying his troops. LEO is in
his early 40s and has a British accent.)

KING HARRY.
Once more unto the breach, dear friends, once more!
Or close the wall up with our English dead.
In peace there's nothing so becomes a man
As modest stillness and humility,
But when the blast of war blows in our ears,
Then imitate the action of the tiger!!

(HOTSPUR, HENRY's mighty nemesis, played by JACK GABLE,
rushes on out of breath and fresh from fighting. Note: The boys
have conflated two different plays here and I can only assure
you that they're ashamed of it. Note also: "Ha!" denotes a thrust
of the sword and its accompanying shout of valor.)

HOTSPUR. Hold up thy head, vile Scot! Thou art Harry
Monmouth.
KING HARRY. And thou art Hotspur, the rebel lord who comes
To take my throne.
HOTSPUR. A plague on both your houses! Ha! Ha!
KING HARRY. Stay back I say!
HOTSPUR. I will not yield, for now is the winter of thy discontent!
KING HARRY.
And yet tomorrow and tomorrow and tomorrow
Creeps in this petty pace from day to day
To the last syllable of
recorded time! Ha! Ha! Ha!

(They fight, furiously, a pitched battle of swords and bucklers. It is rather thrilling.)

HOTSPUR. A horse, a horse, my kingdom for a horse!

(HARRY's final thrust skewers poor HOTSPUR.)

HOTSPUR. Oh, Harry, thou hast robbed me of my youth!

(HOTSPUR dies.)

KING HARRY... To be or not to be, that is the question.
　　　　　　　　Whether tis nobler in the mind to suffer
　　　　　　　　The slings and arrows of outrageous fortune,
　　　　　　　　Or to take arms against a ...

(LEO notices something in the audience. People are walking out, including one MOOSE named FRANK, who is clattering out of the second row and up the aisle. We can tell that FRANK is a MOOSE from the Fez he wears. [FRANK is doubled by the actor who plays BUTCH.] LEO has skipped a beat, but tries to go on, just a little louder.)

KING HARRY. Whether tis nobler in the mind to suffer the slings and arrows of where the hell are they going? They're walking out!

JACK. *(Opening an eye.)* They're heading to the buffet across the hall.

LEO. Hey! Hey! Come back here! What's the matter with you people! We are giving a performance up here!

MOOSE FRANK. *(From the aisle.)* It's boring! Go back where

you came from!

LEO. Oh, really?! Well why don't you go back where you came from?!! Huh?!

MOOSE FRANK. This is where I came from, you idiot. I live here!

LEO. "Idiot?" He called me an "idiot!"

JACK. Leo —

LEO. You're the idiot! You! That's right, you!

MOOSE FRANK. *(Pulling his coat off.)* Want to make something of it, buddy?!

LEO. *(Climbing off the stage.)* By God, I'll knock your block off!

JACK. *(Grabbing him.)* Leo! Leo, stop! STOP IT! *(To MOOSE FRANK:)* He's sorry. Go. Eat. Have a good time. Leo, let's go.

LEO. Ohhh, CRAP! Crap, crap, crap!!!

JACK. *(Shaking his head.)* "Tomorrow and tomorrow and tomorrow ...?"

LEO. *(Rounding on the audience again.)* What's the matter with you people?! Haven't you ever heard of culture?! Huh?! Or civilization?!!

JACK. Leo!

LEO. Next time we'll bring a stripper!

(From the back of the auditorium, the men cheer.)

MEN. *(Off.)* YAY!

(As the boys EXIT, the lights fade quickly and we hear the voice of a TRAIN CONDUCTOR.)

CONDUCTOR. All aboard! Pennsylvania Line, East Coast Local, stopping at Loganville, New Salem, York, Goldsboro, Harrisburg and points North. Please watch your step entering the train. East Coast Local, all aboard!

Scene 3

(The lights come up inside an empty train car the next morning, as JACK and LEO ENTER carrying their suitcases.)

LEO. Morons! They were complete and utter morons!

JACK. Leo —

LEO. What ever happened to respect?! Hmm? And-and-and courtesy?! I mean, didn't they even look at our flyers?! I put them in the lobby. With our best reviews! "Mesmerizing."

JACK. The Mecklenberg Ledger.

LEO. "Fascinating."

JACK. The Beaver Falls Dispatch.

LEO. *(Glares at JACK.)* "A powerhouse night of theatre." The New York Times.

JACK. You made that one up.

LEO. Yes, I know, but it was on the flyer!

JACK. Leo, do you really want to do Shakespeare all your life?

LEO. Yes! I spent three years at the Royal Academy of Dramatic Art.

JACK. You told me you went there to meet women.

LEO. I did, but then I got interested. God, just look at us! It's been ten years and we're still at the bottom. Rock bottom! I can feel my arse scraping on the little stones ...

JACK. Do you know what I want? I mean really want? *(He's deadly serious now.)* Neighbors. A house. People who care if I open the front door in the morning.

LEO. Well... of course... But Jack we can still make it! As actors! All we need is a break! *(Suddenly galvanized, turning on a dime.)* And we're in luck. Finally! This morning I read in Variety that MGM is doing a movie version of Julius Caesar. In Los Angeles. They have James Mason as Brutus, John Gielgud as Cassius, and they're looking for more Shakespearean actors. This is made for us. I mean, how many Shakespearean actors do they have in America? Six? Now, how much do we have in the kitty? For the flight — as of right now?

JACK. Leo, we can't afford it.

LEO. Don't be negative! Just tell me. How much have we saved?

JACK. You don't want to know.

LEO. A thousand? Eight hundred. Six. Five? How much?!

JACK. Nothing.

LEO. No really.

JACK. We don't have a dime.

LEO. *(In shock.)* But — but — what about last night? Our show for the moose people?

JACK. They wouldn't pay us.

LEO. What?!

JACK. I went right up to the Great Yak. He said six of his members resigned at the buffet. One more soliloquy, he would have lost the herd.

LEO. Those... cheaters! Those-those-those crooks.

JACK. Maybe we should do a whole play next time, like we used to.

LEO. Oh, oh, oh that's a great idea! Except we have no actors, it's just the two of us! We have seven costumes! From different plays! In a pinch we could put on "One Gentleman of Verona!" "The Taming of the Merry Wife of Windsor!"

JACK. All right, all right...

LEO. "Much Ado About Hamlet!"

JACK. All right!

LEO. I just... I... I mean it's... it's just...

(He's in despair. Real despair. JACK feels awful for him.)

JACK. Would you like some breakfast? Maybe they have a café car.

LEO. *(Bitterly.)* We can't afford it. Remember?

JACK. I lied. I have a dollar left. It's on me.

(JACK EXITS. LEO is alone and despondent. After a moment, he notices a local newspaper on the train seat across the aisle. The York Dispatch. He picks it up and glances at the front page. Then something catches his eye and he reads more carefully. The more he reads, the more absorbed he becomes. The story continues on the inside, and when he opens the paper, we see the headline on the front page: "Oh Max, Oh Steve!" JACK re-ENTERS.)

JACK. I can't believe it! They want a dollar-fifty for two eggs!

LEO. Jack, take a look at this.

JACK. It's highway robbery!

LEO. It's important. Look. "Oh Max, Oh Steve." "Dying Woman Seeks Loved Ones. Large Fortune At Stake." Listen! "Millionairess Florence Snider of York, Pennsylvania, is reported to be searching desperately for her sister's children, Max and Steve, to whom she intends to leave the bulk of her fortune."

JACK. I think I have some extra change some place ...

LEO. "Miss Snider last saw Max and Steve when, as children, they sailed for England with their mother. She corresponded for a time, but then lost all contact —"

LEADING LADIES

JACK. Would you get to the point, I'm hungry!

LEO. The boys went to England. They left here as children. Listen: "Repeated telegrams and advertisements in America and England have failed to get a response." She can't find them! And apart from a niece named... Meg who lives with her in York, she wants to leave them her money.

JACK. So what?

LEO. So what?! Jack, what are we? You and I. Are we Polish?

JACK. No.

LEO. Hungarian?

JACK. No.

LEO. Lithuanian?

JACK. No.

LEO. We're English! We have English accents! And look at us! We could be brothers. We even look alike. *(He holds JACK around the shoulders and they look out at the audience. They look nothing at all alike, of course.)* You could be Steve and I could be Max.

JACK. Us? Her nephews?

LEO. Bingo.

JACK. But we're not her nephews. It's a lie.

LEO. Not necessarily. Do you know all your relations?

JACK. Oh, stop it. I can't pretend to be somebody else. Besides which, it's illegal. They could put us in jail!

LEO. Jack, Florence Snider has tried for months to reach her nephews and she can't find them. So we wouldn't be hurting anybody. Do you think that I would hurt anybody?

JACK. What about the niece? Meg.

LEO. The hell with her. She'll get plenty. Look, it says the estate is estimated at three million dollars. So instead of three million, she gets one million. And you get a million and I get a million.

JACK. A million dollars?

LEO. *(Emotionally.)* We could start over. Try again... from the beginning... become something...

JACK. Leo ...

LEO. Jack, please.

JACK. But she could have seen pictures of her nephews! In the past couple of months!

LEO. I've thought of that, so we don't show up until she kicks the bucket.

JACK. Dead?

LEO. No, Jack, a little wooden bucket that she kicks on its side ... Yes of course dead! We wait nearby and keep our ears to the ground. The minute she goes, we send a telegram.

JACK. It won't work.

LEO. Yes it will.

JACK. No it won't! We don't know anything about Max and Steve! How old they are. When they left. Their mother's name. Their father's name. We'd have to know somebody from York, Pennsylvania!

(At this moment, AUDREY skates in on roller skates. She's wearing a brightly colored uniform with a matching hat. She also carries some text books and a towel. She's about 20, extremely well-built and extremely sweet and good-natured. She's a knockout.)

AUDREY. Wheeee!

(As she skates in, she can't stop herself and careens right into JACK, who catches her.)

AUDREY. Oh, thanks! *(For JACK, it's love at first sight.)* Hi. I bet you're wondering why I'm dressed up like this.

JACK. It's very cheerful.

AUDREY. It's my first day at the Tastee Bite. See? "Tastee Bite."

(She points to her chest, and her tight sweater has the words "Tastee Bite" across the front.)

LEO. The first E gets a bit lost in the middle.

AUDREY. I took the training course yesterday and I passed with flying colors. They said I had the best potential of anybody they interviewed since they opened their doors to the public!

JACK. When did they open?

AUDREY. Monday.

JACK. Good show.

AUDREY. They have faith in me and that counts for a lot. Right?

LEO. Absolutely.

AUDREY. To tell you the truth, I got the job just to make some money. I want to go to college. Ergo, the books. Ergo means therefore. I mean, I know it's a commute and all, living in York, but I figure it's worth it if it helps get me through college.

LEO. ... You live in York?

AUDREY. Yeah.

LEO. York, Pennsylvania?

AUDREY. Yeah.

LEO. You wouldn't know a Miss Florence Snider by any chance?

AUDREY. Are you kidding me? When I worked for a doctor, she came to the office like every day.

LEO. Do you know when she last saw "Max" and "Steve?"

AUDREY. 1920.

LEO. How old they were?

AUDREY. Six and four.

LEO. Their mother's name?

AUDREY. Jennie.

LEO. Father's?

AUDREY. Irv.

LEO. Yes!

JACK. Oh, no.

AUDREY. I remember when she used to come to the office, everything with her was a big deal. If she had a headache, it was a migraine, she had a slight fever, she was burning up. She was always exaggerating.

LEO. And how's she doing?

AUDREY. She's dead. She died this morning.

JACK. Oh, crap!

AUDREY. I know. It's awful.

LEO. What about Max and Steve? Has anyone heard from them?

AUDREY. Nope, not a word. The funny thing is, she didn't even have a picture of them. I asked her. She was real broken up about it. She said she thought that the older one, that was Max, she thought that Max was in the theatre.

LEO. In the theatre ...!

JACK. Oh, God..

LEO. Ha! Fate! Providence! "If it be now, 'tis not to come; if it be not to come, it will be now; if it be not now, yet it will come. The readiness is all!"

AUDREY. Yeah. ... Anyway, I feel bad for her. I found her very congenial. That means nice. One day she comes in and I'm helping her up the stairs and she says "I'm gonna remember you in my will," and I say, "Do it with money" — teasing her, you know? And she says "You should live so long," which I thought was nice, her wanting me to live a long time.

LEO. Is there anything else she ever said about Max and Steve? Anything distinctive about them? A scar, a limp ...

AUDREY. Nope. Not really. Just average normal people. She said that Steve was deaf and dumb, but that's about all.

LEO. Deaf and dumb?

AUDREY. Yeah. It's congenital. Not to be confused with congenial. Can I leave my stuff here? I gotta practice my skating. See, to work at this place you've got to roller skate from table to table. I still need some practice, but I've got a plan. The aisles. See? They're nice and straight. And they're numerous, which means there's a lot of them, and they're contiguous, which means that one comes right after the other in a straight line, like two worms sucking each other's lips. My name's Audrey.

JACK. Jack. Jack Gable. Like Clark Gable without the cleft in the chin.

AUDREY. Hey, You're cute. I'll see ya later!

(She skates off.)

JACK. She thinks I'm cute ...

LEO. Fine, you're cute. And you'll be deaf and dumb and I'll do all the talking.

JACK. Oh, stop it.

LEO. Why not? It's perfect!

JACK. I can't be deaf and dumb, I-I-I don't know any sign language.

LEO. So you'll make it up! It's easy!

JACK. It is not!

LEO. Of course it is! Try it! Just try it! Say... "yes." *(Reluctantly, Jack hold his hands out facing each other, fingers up and extended, the hands parallel.)* Say "no." *(JACK crosses his hands.)* "Maybe." *(Wavy hand.)* "I'm hungry." *(Points to his mouth with his tongue out.)* "I'm thirsty." *(Swigs, using his thumb as a bottle.)* "I have an idea." *(Finger up with a big smile.)* All right, good. *(Still signing, Jack gives a silent thumbs up.)* Stop it. *(JACK signs "stop it" by putting his palms face down and tossing them to the sides, the way an umpire indicates "safe" in baseball.)* Stop doing that, Jack. *(JACK does the "stop it" sign and points to himself.)* It isn't funny!

(JACK does the "stop it" sign, then imitates laughing.)

JACK. Oh. Sorry. I'm sure it's not real sign language.

LEO. We'll tell them it's a new system. Signing for the simple. We'll say you can't hear a thing. You read lips, but only mine. Now the problem is that Audrey lives in York and she heard you talking just now. So you'll have to wear a beard or something to play Steve. So she doesn't recognize you.

JACK. I look terrible in a beard!

LEO. That's not the point! Now what have we got?

(He rummages through JACK's costume bag and pulls out a beard.)

LEO. Try this.
JACK. No.
LEO. Just try it!
JACK. It looks fake.

(JACK tries on the beard.)

LEO. Try it with this hat. *(LEO pulls out JACK's Polonius head-covering and JACK pulls it on.)* That's better. Now what about these glasses. *(LEO pulls out a pair of glasses and JACK puts them on.)* Good.

(At which moment, AUDREY skates back in. JACK is petrified; LEO recovers quickly.)

AUDREY. *(Off, then on.)* Whee! Hi. Sorry. I forgot my towel

... *(She sees JACK and is startled.)* Hey! Did he have a beard just now?

LEO. Who? Him? I-I don't think you've met him.

AUDREY. I haven't?

LEO. No. Oh, oh, of course. You met Jack, an old friend. This is my brother Steve.

AUDREY. "Steve?" No kidding. Hi. How are ya?

LEO. I'm afraid he can't hear what you're saying. He's deaf and dumb.

AUDREY. Deaf and d -! Holy cow! That's incredible! Usually I never even hear about anybody being deaf and dumb, now it comes up twice. Talk about a coincidence!

LEO. Ah, but is it? You see, this is Steve. And I'm his brother.

AUDREY. I know. It's amazing. Two deaf people named Steve.

LEO. Two...?

AUDREY. Yeah. Don't you remember? Max and Steve. The two girls we talked about. Like I told you, the younger one is deaf and dumb.

LEO. "Two girls?"

AUDREY. Yeah.

LEO. But ... Max and Steve are men, aren't they?

AUDREY. No. Oh oh oh! I get it! I bet you got mixed up because of their names, right? But they're not men, they're girls! Their real names are Maxine and Stephanie.

JACK. "Maxine and Stephanie?" Oh that's great, that is just great!

AUDREY. Hey, he just talked.

LEO. Amazing are you absolutely sure they're girls?

AUDREY. Sure. I talked to Miss Snider like a hundred times about them.

LEO. It didn't say they were girls in the paper.

AUDREY. I'll bet you just missed it. Most people don't read

carefully.

JACK. Quite right, here it is. It says girls. Right here. Look. "Girls!"

AUDREY. You know, he talks very well for a beginner. Well, if you'll excuse me, I'm gonna go practice my skating. *(TO JACK.)* CONGRATULATIONS. YOU'RE MAKING TERRIFIC PROGRESS.

JACK. Thank you.

(She skates away.)

LEO. God damn it, God damn it! We were so close! I could taste it! With two million dollars, we could have made our own Shakespeare movie!

JACK. At least I can talk now.

LEO. GOOOODDDDAAMMMITT! *(In a rage, LEO throws one of the suitcases on the floor — and it springs open, sending costumes spilling everywhere.)* Oh, great. Just look at this. Costumes, to remind me of our latest defeat.

JACK. I'll help, I'll help. *(As they begin gathering up the costumes, LEO holds up a wig and a dress and looks at them quizzically. Meanwhile, JACK is holding a gown up to himself.)* Ha. Remember this one? Juliet. We had that knockout actress and I used to say, "Pardon me, but would you like to climb up my balcony ...?" Ha. And look at this. The Taming of the Shrew. "If I be waspish, best beware my sting."

(He holds the dress in front of him and models it, chuckling. Then he notices LEO. LEO's mind is grinding away. He's getting a maniacal look in his eyes. He stares at the dress in his own hands, then looks back at JACK.)

LEO. "If it be now, 'tis not to come; if it be not to come, it will be now —"

JACK. No.

LEO. Yes.

JACK. No!

LEO. We can do it! It'll work! I'll be Maxine, you'll be Stephanie.

JACK. Wrong! I will not dress up as a woman. Ever. I don't do that.

LEO. For a million dollars? The question is, which dress do you wear.

(LEO starts rummaging through the suitcase, tossing costumes in all directions.)

JACK. NO. HEY. WOULD YOU STOP IT?! HEY CUT THAT OUT! RIGHT NOW! JUST STOP IT!

LEO. Ooh, ooh, ooh, I think I'd look good in this one. Cleopatra, Queen of the Nile.

JACK. You'd look ridiculous!

LEO. Now what about you ...?

JACK. I am not doing this. Do you hear me? ARE YOU LISTENING?!

LEO. What about this? It has a plunging neckline —

JACK. They wouldn't believe me! I'm not a good actor!

LEO. You get very good reviews.

JACK. BECAUSE YOU WRITE THEM!

LEO. *(Holding up a diaphanous number.)* Ooh, ooh, ooh, look at this. It's perfect. Titania, Queen of the Fairies.

JACK. I can't wear that! It has wings on it!

LEO. We'll cut them off.

JACK. No!

LEO. Jack, don't you remember the good old days. We said we could do anything. And we believed it! You played Richard the Third with that big hump on your back, and you hobbled around the stage like some deranged homunculus. You played Romeo and bounded gracefully onto Juliet's balcony. You brought the house down.

JACK. I brought the balcony down.

LEO. Just that one night.

JACK. But Leo, those were all men! I can't play a woman!

LEO. Why not?

JACK. Because I'm a chap, a bloke, a guy!

LEO. Jack! Who do you think played the women's roles in Shakespeare's time? Huh?

JACK. Chaps?

LEO. Exactly. And how did they do it?

JACK. Small brassieres?

LEO. They did it with conviction. With sheer talent. Because they were actors, like you and me. And if this works, we can be successful actors. We can start over. Go to Los Angeles. Get another chance. Jack, it's the role of lifetime. Will you meet the challenge? Will you rise to the occasion? Will you fulfill your destiny and save your best friend from a life of crushing disappointment and defeat? Yes or no?!

JACK. NO!

LEO. I'll take that as a yes. Now we'll get off at the next stop, send them a telegram, get into our costumes, get back on the train and then it's on to York, Pennsylvania! Ha ha!

(Blackout.)

LEADING LADIES

Scene 4

(We hear a telephone ring and the lights come up on DUNCAN and MEG, in separate places, on the phone with each other. MEG has placed the call and DUNCAN is answering it. MEG is bright-eyed with excitement, and can't wait to tell DUNCAN her news.)

DUNCAN. Hello. Evangelical United Bretheren Church of York. Reverend Wooley speaking.

MEG. Duncan, it's me! Guess what?! A telegram just arrived and guess who it's from. And don't say Grandma Kunkle.

DUNCAN. Winston Churchill.

MEG. Wrong. It's from Max and Steve!

DUNCAN. Max and Steve?

MEG. Yes! Isn't it wonderful! I have cousins! They arrive today at 5:30. And I've never even met them. Isn't it exciting?!

DUNCAN. Yes it is, my goodness, but... You do realize this means you'll have to split your inheritance.

MEG. Well of course.

DUNCAN. Instead of three million, you'll only get one million.

MEG. A million dollars is enough for ten lifetimes. And you always say yourself that money isn't important.

DUNCAN. Well it isn't. Per se. But one can do so much good with three million dollars. I could set up a foundation. And run it from a nice new office. I'd interview charities that ask me for grant money. They'd take me to lunch and try to woo me ...

MEG. Or we could give it all away in one big lump and just go on living the way things are.

DUNCAN. Now that's ridiculous! It would be vain and boast-ful.

MEG. Oh, Duncan. You were counting on all three million,

weren't you.

DUNCAN. Yes, I was. But not for myself. For the foundation.

MEG. And for that little house on Nantucket.

DUNCAN. Well we'd have to run it out of some place.

MEG. They arrive on the six o'clock train.

DUNCAN. Very fortuitous, their arriving this week. And then one has to ask if it's entirely by chance.

MEG. What do you mean?

DUNCAN. Have you ever thought that they might be frauds.

MEG. Oh, stop it.

DUNCAN. Why not? I mean it's a very convenient time to arrive. They will get two million dollars.

MEG. Would you please forget about the money.

DUNCAN. I am not thinking about the money! I told you that. But maybe they're not

BOTH. as Christian as we are.

MEG. Duncan, you're becoming awfully intolerant.

DUNCAN. Nonsense.

MEG. You know what God thinks of intolerant people.

DUNCAN. Meg —

MEG. One minute you're brushing your teeth, then whammo, you're a pillar of salt.

DUNCAN. Meg!

MEG. With greedy people it's even worse.

DUNCAN. I am not greedy! ... Look. We'll all be very happy to meet your cousins. That's all that matters.

MEG. You will be here when they arrive, won't you? I want to meet them on the platform.

DUNCAN. I'll try. But we have a Boy Scout meeting here at five and I'm handing out the merit badges. It's very exciting. One of the boys is making Eagle, and we have two Hawks and a Pigeon, so I'd better go now and get ready.

MEG. All right, see you later.
DUNCAN. Kiss kiss.

(They hang up.)

Scene 5

(The actions shifts to the living room of FLORENCE Snider's house, a half hour later. DOCTOR MEYERS and his son BUTCH are hanging a banner that reads: "Welcome Max and Steve." Butch, early 20s, is a little slow on the uptake, but earnest and sincere, with a good heart. He played football in high school. DOC and Butch argue a lot and adore each other.)

DOC. Butch, I want you to listen to me and keep an open mind! All right?! Are we clear on this?!

BUTCH. Yes, Father.

DOC. The point I'm making is: It's just as easy to go to bed with a rich girl as it

BOTH. *(Simultaneously.)* is a poor one.

BUTCH. Father!

DOC. The two women coming off that train will be rich as Croesus. Marry one and you'll be set for life.

BUTCH. But I'm in love with Audrey!

DOC. Butch! Sow your oats, by all means. Plow the field, till the soil, water the fruit, but marry for cash.

BUTCH. Oh, Father ...

DOC. Look at me, Butch. I'm not joking! I married for love. Biggest mistake I ever made in my whole life. You could have had

Meg, for God's sake! Before she got engaged to our anal-retentive minister.

BUTCH. Father, Meg is my best friend!

DOC. People do stay friends after they're married, Butch. I read about them in a book once!

(MEG ENTERS, hurrying down the stairs and DOC stomps off to the other side of the room. MEG has smartened up for the arrival of her cousins and wears a twin set.)

BUTCH. Hey, Meg.

MEG. What's eating him?

BUTCH. He doesn't like Audrey. He thinks I should marry a girl with deeper pockets, like one of your cousins coming off the train.

(MEG sighs. Here we go again.)

MEG. Butch, are you in love with Audrey?

BUTCH. I think so.

MEG. How does she make you feel?

BUTCH. Happy.

MEG. And how do you make her feel?

BUTCH. Happy.

MEG. And what do you want to do about it?

BUTCH. Sleep with her.

MEG. What else do you want to do about it?

BUTCH. Marry her.

MEG. Well what are you waiting for, a comet?!

(DUNCAN ENTERS from the front hall.)

DUNCAN. Well, well, well. Greetings all.

DOC. Well look who's here. It's the Reverend Do-gooder.

DUNCAN. And good afternoon to you, Doctor Death. Killed any patients yet today?

DOC. No, but I did enjoy your sermon on Sunday. Best sleep I've had in weeks. Awhooo!

(The call of the MOOSE.)

MEG. Would you two stop it. Duncan, we've got to hurry. We're going to be late.

DUNCAN. You're rushing me again, my dear. Now please. Nothing profits from haste.

MEG. Yes, Duncan, but did I tell you that Maxine is in the theatre? She's an actress!

DUNCAN. Yes, you did, though personally I can't imagine why anyone would voluntarily put on a silly costume, stand up in front of a lot of people and pontificate about something that most of the audience has absolutely no interest in.

BUTCH... You're a minister. Don't you do that?

MEG. Wait. Oh, no. I forgot the flowers. Oh, darn it! I'll be right back!

(She dashes up the stairs and disappears into her room.)

DUNCAN. Haste, haste ...

DOC & DUNCAN. Nothing profits from haste.

DOC. You told us that, you jackass.

(At this moment, AUDREY hurries in from the garden, wild with excitement.)

AUDREY. Hey! Hey! Everybody, guess what, guess what?!

BUTCH. Hey, Audrey. How was your first day?

AUDREY. Great, Butch, thanks, but listen —

BUTCH. I love you with roller skates. They really set off your eyes.

AUDREY. Thanks, now listen! Guess who's coming?!

BUTCH. Maxine and Stephanie.

AUDREY. How did you know?

DOC. We got a telegram this afternoon.

DUNCAN. They're due any time now.

AUDREY. "Due any time?" They're outside!! I just met 'em and they're comin' up the path!! And let me tell you, English girls are a whole other thing. These are not your ordinary women. I'll bring 'em in! *(Calling.)* Hey! This way! Come on, don't be shy.

(LEO and JACK ENTER, dressed as women. LEO wears the dress of Cleopatra of the Nile. JACK's Titania dress still has wings on it. LEO, as MAXINE, is chic and flamboyant. JACK, as STEPHANIE, is shy and demure. BUTCH, DUNCAN and DOC stare gaping at them, their mouths hanging open. AUDREY looks proud. Of course, whenever LEO speaks as MAXINE, he uses a feminine, high-pitched voice.)

LEO. Hello, hello, hello, my darlings! Oh! How wonderful to arrive at long last into the bosom of my own dear family. "Oh! This blessed plot, this earth, this realm, this York, P-A."

(LEO beams. JACK looks terrified.)

BUTCH. Are you really Maxine and Stephanie?

LEO. No, I'm just Maxine. This is Stephanie. *(He holds JACK's fingers to his lips.)* Stephanie, say hello to the nice people.

(JACK bows upstage in both directions, giving us a clear view of the back of his dress — which still has two fairy wings sticking out. At this moment, MEG hurries down the stairs, carrying flowers.)

MEG. Oh, I'm sorry! I'm sorry I'm late, I'm AH! *(The sight of them startles her. To AUDREY:)* Is this ...? *(Audrey nods.)* ... Here. These flowers are for you. I'm your cousin Margaret.

(LEO stops dead. He's dumbstruck. She's the most beautiful girl he's ever seen.)

LEO. How... how... how do you do? Auntie Florence never told us you were so... beautiful.

(LEO stares at her, unable to move. MEG wants to embrace them, but hesitates... then, with a cry of happiness, she gives in to her affectionate nature and gives them each a hug. The very touch of her makes LEO dizzy.)

MEG. Oh, I am so happy to meet you! Let me introduce you to my friends. This is our Pastor, Reverend Wooley.
DUNCAN. How do you do.'
LEO. Ah, I see that you're a man of the cloth. I find that so inspiring, so je ne sais quoi. Do you speak French?
DUNCAN. No.
LEO. Anyone? *(Everyone murmurs no.)* Ah, que jamais tout de suite à Sorbonne à la frommage et bon soir. Next.
MEG. This is Doctor Meyers, who has taken such wonderful care of Aunt Florence.
LEO. How good of you to bother.

DOC. If you ever need an operation, just call me. I do plastic surgery on the side.

LEO. But I don't need it on my side, it's my face that ... Oh, ha! Next.

MEG. This is Butch. And Audrey.

BUTCH. She's my girlfriend. We're going to be married soon!

DOC. Over my dead body.

LEO. And wouldn't that make an unusual ceremony. "Do you take this woman, standing on this dead body, to be your ... Ha!"

AUDREY. *(Putting JACK's fingers to her lips.)* WELCOME TO OUR METROPOLIS! THAT MEANS CITY!

(JACK hugs her warmly, rocking back and forth.)

AUDREY. Aww ...

LEO. How sweet. *(JACK does it again.)* Such an affectionate little thing... *(Again.)* That's enough!... Now could you possibly take us to see dear Auntie Florence?

MEG. Well ...

LEO. What? Oh, no! I can see it in your face. We aren't too late, are we?

MEG. Maxine ...

LEO. Oh, no, no, no!

MEG. Maxine ...

LEO. I can't believe it! After all this time! Stephanie! Stephanie, listen to me! *(Fingers to lips.)* We're too late! Auntie Florence is dead!

(JACK opens his mouth and screams in complete silence. He looks like Edvard Munch's "The Scream," but rocking back and forth, arms up.)

MEG. Maxine! You're not too late! She isn't dead!

(LEO and JACK stop cold. They look at each other in horror.)

LEO... Not dead?
MEG. No. She's hanging on. And she wants to see you.
LEO. But-but-but-
AUDREY. Butch, this morning you told me she was dead!
BUTCH. That's what Father said.
DOC. She had no pulse! Then she got better! What do you want from me?!

(LEO and JACK start sneaking away.)

MEG. Maxine? Where are you going?
LEO. The news. It's overwhelming. We thought a little stroll might help us recover ...

(A voice from off stage is heard, and LEO and JACK freeze.)

FLORENCE. *(Off.)* Are they here?! Where are they?! I want to see them!

(AUNT FLORENCE ENTERS. She's very old, extremely crusty, and her eyesight is terrible.)

MEG. Aunt Florence! You should be in bed!
FLORENCE. *(All sweetness.)* Don't be ridiculous. I have two little nieces to meet. Where are they? ... *(Tough and angry!)* WHERE ARE THEY?!
MEG. Right over here.
FLORENCE. Maxine? Stephanie?

LEO. Yes?

(She scrutinizes them; a tense moment.)

FLORENCE. *(Crying.)*...They're so beautiful! Maxine, my darling, it's really you...

LEO. Auntie Florence, dear Auntie Florence... You look so wealthy... healthy! So rich in color. So loaded with charm. "Age cannot wither her, nor custom stale her infinite variety."

FLORENCE. That must be Stephanie.

LEO. No, it's Shakespeare. Wait. Stephanie doesn't know yet. She thinks you're dead. *(Fingers to lips.)* Stephanie. Brace yourself. This is your Auntie Florence.

(JACK does another toreador flourish. Then he does some signing that clearly says "Let's get the hell out of here.")

LEO. Yes, I agree. As soon as possible. She says it can't be Auntie Florence, you look so young.

FLORENCE. Oh, the sweet baby!

(She pulls Jack fiercely to her bosom.)

DOC. Florence, you should be in bed.

FLORENCE. Oh be quiet, murderer. You said I was dead. I could have been buried alive.

DOC. I made a mistake. It happens. You don't make mistakes?

FLORENCE. Not like that I don't.

DOC. What about your stock tips? Huh?! They all stunk!

FLORENCE. That's different! They don't kill people!

DOC. They all went straight down the toilet!

FLORENCE. IT'S NOT THE SAME THING!

(And with that, AUNT FLORENCE grabs her chest and starts to gasp.)

FLORENCE. Argh!
MEG. Aunt Florence!
FLORENCE. Argh!
BUTCH. I've got her! I've got her!
AUDREY. Florence!
DOC. Oh, damn. Get her inside.
MEG. Maxine, we'll be right back. She should be fine, don't worry.
LEO. Can I help?
MEG. No, it's okay, really. We put a bedroom on the ground floor. I'll be right back!

(Everyone helps FLORENCE off, leaving LEO and JACK alone.)

JACK. All right, now let's get the hell out of here!
LEO. Wait. Wait. Wait! Not yet! I think we should stay.
JACK. Stay? Are you crazy?!
LEO. Jack, this whole thing could still work. I mean, why not?
JACK. Because she's still alive. And she's really mean!
LEO. But she can't last much longer. She must be a thousand years old.
JACK. She could linger. Old people do that, they linger out of spite.
LEO. I say we give it a couple of weeks.
JACK. A couple of weeks?!
LEO. Shh!
JACK. Are you crazy?! Look at me! I have wings on! I feel like I'm in "Charley's Aunt Meets the Fairy Queen!" And where the hell

did this "Maxine" creature come from?!

LEO. *(Worried.)* I have no idea.

JACK. She's from another planet. She's possessing you. It's like "The Invasion of the Body Snatchers!"

LEO. Look, how about this. We take it a day at a time. We spend the night, and if they get suspicious, we reconsider.

JACK. No.

LEO. It's worth it, Jack.

JACK. No!

LEO. Two million dollars!

JACK. No!

LEO. Jack! *(MEG REENTERS.)* be nimble, Jack be quick, Jack jump over Hello, you're back, you're back!

MEG. Am I interrupting?

LEO. No, no, no, no, no, no! You're just in time. *(Hand to lips:)* Yes, Stephanie, of course you can take a stroll. Why don't you get one of those train schedules from the station. Then we'll know what time the little trainies leave from here to go to other places. It might come in handy if we're ever in a hurry. Who knows?

(LEO laughs gaily. JACK signs "All right, but I don't like it!" and EXITS.)

LEO. Now how is dear Auntie Florence doing?

MEG. I'm afraid it doesn't look very good. It's been like this for months. But at least you made it before anything happened. She got to see you after all these years. That means a great deal to all of us.

LEO. Thank you.

MEG. But ... oh I don't know how to put this... could you tell me just one thing? About yourself.

LEO. *(Worried.)* Yes, I-I suppose so ...

LEADING LADIES

MEG. It doesn't really matter at all, and I don't mean to pry.

LEO. No, please. Go ahead.

MEG. Well... is it true that you're really... in the theatre?

LEO. The thea... Oh, oh, oh yes! Yes, I am. Absolutely.

MEG. Oh, I think that's so wonderful! My happiest memory in the world is when my father took me to Philadelphia to see my first Shakespeare. It was Twelfth Night, my favorite.

LEO. *(Stunned.)*... My senior project at the Royal Academy was Twelfth Night.

MEG. The Royal Academy of Dramatic Art? In London? Oh God, you're my hero!

LEO. I am?

MEG. Can I tell you a secret? If I could do anything in the whole world, I mean if somehow things changed like magic, overnight, all I'd ever want to do is be an actress. I'd want to recite Shakespeare every night and let those words just tumble out of me like a waterfall. I'd want to play Rosalind and Juliet and Cleopatra. Do you specialize in anything?

LEO. Specialize?

MEG. You know, comedy, tragedy ...?

LEO. Oh, I do a bit of everything. Comedy. Tragedy. Comical-tragedy. "Tragical-comical-historical-pastoral, scene individual or poem unlimited." I did a Command Performance of Twelfth Night not long ago for the Queen of England.

MEG. What did you play?

LEO. The Duke Orsino! ...'sssss lady love, the fair Olivia.

MEG. Oh my God, I'd give anything to have seen you in it. Do some for me. Would you? Just a little?

LEO. Now?

MEG. Yes!

LEO. Oh I couldn't.

MEG. Please!

LEO. You embarrass me.

MEG. A few lines. Please! I know it all by heart. I'll do Viola's lines. She's my favorite character in all the plays. "What I am, and what I would, are as secret as maidenhead: to your ears, divinity, to any other's profanation. Good madam, let me see your face."

(Note: this is one of the sexiest and most romantic passages in all of Shakespeare. LEO plays Olivia to the hilt. He's a grande dame, vain and resplendent. The tone shifts at MEG's speech "With adorations, with fertile tears," and from that point on, the tone is lushly romantic.)

LEO. "Have you any commission from your lord to negotiate with my face? You are now out of your text. But we will draw the curtain and show you the picture." *(She unveils and shows her face.)* "Look you, sir. Is't not well done?"

MEG. "Excellently done, if God did all."

LEO. "'Tis in grain, sir, 'twill endure wind and weather."

MEG. O, if I did love you in my master's flame,

With such a suff'ring, such a deadly life,

In your denial I would find no sense,

I would not understand it."

LEO. "Why, what would you?"

MEG. "Make me a willow cabin at your gate

And call upon my soul within the house,

Write loyal cantons of contemnèd love,

And sing them loud even in the dead of night;

Halloo your name to the reverberate hills,

And make the babbling gossip of the air

Cry out "Olivia!"

(Silence. LEO is so smitten he can barely speak.)

LEO. ... We should get married.

MEG. What?

LEO. You. You should get married. Are you married?

MEG. No. I'm not.

LEO. Oh good! Isn't that splendid.

MEG. But I'm getting married next month.

(LEO turns white and he almost falls.)

LEO. What? You are? Next month?

MEG. That's right.

LEO. But-but-but you haven't met me yet!

MEG. I'm sorry?

LEO. Met-met-met-me. To met-me. It's an Old English expression. It means to live life to the fullest. From the French, metmoyer. And who exactly is the lucky man?

MEG. You met him just now. Duncan. Reverend Wooley.

LEO. Him? Reverend Woo — But-but my dear, you... you don't have an engagement ring.

MEG. Duncan says that rings are earthly symbols of material wealth.

LEO. You mean he's cheap. And where's the honeymoon?

MEG. He doesn't believe in honeymoons, either. But can I tell you a secret? Some day I want to go to Paris.

LEO. Well of course you do. And you should want to. But are you in love with Reverend Whosits?

MEG. *(Taken aback.)* Wooley. Yes, of course I am. You see, he was friends with my mother and father, here in York, and they passed away when I was young. And he was very kind when they died, and helped me get through it. And so it means a lot to me. That we can talk about them.

LEO. Ah.

MEG. I think that's what love is, don't you? Having something you can share, then letting it grow.

LEO. No, no, no, no, no! My dear, love is lightning. It makes you ache and cry and laugh and scream. It lingers your desire and makes you count the minutes till your wedding night so that your heart stops beating with the anticipation of it.

MEG. *(In awe.)*... Have you ever been in love like that?

LEO. Oh, yes... But what am I saying? I'm interfering and I shouldn't. I wish you every happiness in the world with that man. Duncan. Reverend Woolsack.

MEG. Thank you. You will be here for the wedding, won't you? Oh please say yes! It's three weeks from Sunday.

LEO. Well, I'm afraid that all depends. I may have to... meet someone in New York. A very dear friend of mine. Leo Clark. One of the greatest actors in the English-speaking world. I'm sure you've heard of him.

MEG. Yes, I have!

LEO. You have?

MEG. I saw him about two years ago in Philadelphia doing Scenes from Shakespeare. He was wonderful! I fell in love with him! Is he your boyfriend?

LEO. Hm? No. No! Not at all. We're just very close. Inseparable, you might say.

MEG. This is so amazing. I was supposed to go see him last night. In Shrewsbury. Which is only 20 miles from here. In fact, you could go visit him right now, unless... Maxine?... Hello?

(But MAXINE is lost in thought.)

LEO. I wonder ...
MEG. What?

LEO. Shh! Don't interrupt. *(Silence.)* ... I am getting the most marvelous idea. Margaret, what if Leo Clark came here to meet you ... and the two of you put on a performance of Shakespeare, together.

MEG. ... You're teasing me.

LEO. I am not, now listen. You get married in just three and a half weeks. Right? So, in honor of your wedding, we plan a special event to make it truly unforgettable: a scene from Shakespeare — no! a whole play — Twelfth Night — starring you and Leo Clark.

MEG. You are teasing me!

LEO. No I am not! Look, Leo is close by. You are my cousin. And I would love the two of you to spend some time together ...

MEG. Well first of all, he wouldn't do it.

LEO. Of course he would! He's devoted to me!

MEG. But he'll be too busy! He must work all the time!

LEO. Well, not all the time.

MEG. But he wouldn't do it with me! I'm not a real actress! I'm not good enough!

LEO. Nonsense.

MEG. I'm not!

LEO. Margaret, I just heard you! You were marvelous!

MEG. But I have no training.

LEO. So he'll give you lessons! Private acting lessons! And you'll spend a lot of time together! — which believe me, he wouldn't mind at all.

MEG. Oh he'd hate that.

LEO. He would kill for it.

MEG. But —

LEO. Margaret. Didn't you tell me not five minutes ago that you would love to be an actress? More than anything in the world? Well here's your chance — and believe me, it isn't every day that chances — any chances — come along. Do it now, before life gets cold.

MEG. .... All right, I'll do it.

LEO. That's my girl!

MEG. Eeeeee! Oh my God. I can't believe it. And listen! Aunt Florence is giving a party the night before the wedding. We could do the performance then.

LEO. Well that's perfection!

MEG. But it won't interfere with the wedding, will it? I mean, you don't think Duncan will mind, do you?

LEO. Noooooo. Of course not.

MEG. Eeeee! This is incredible! Leo Clark!

LEO. Yes? ... Oh, yes! Leo Clark. The Leo Clark.

MEG. The New York Times called him "a living legend." It was on one of his flyers.

LEO. Yes, I remember that one ...

MEG. So you'll call him?

LEO. Who?

MEG. Mr. Clark.

LEO. Oh, yes yes yes. No problem. Leave it all to me.

MEG. All right. *(Pause.)* Would you like to see your room now? You must be exhausted.

LEO. I think I'll wait here for Stephanie. If that's all right.

MEG. Oh yes.

LEO. You're sure?

MEG. Of course. Anything you want.

LEO. Anything?

MEG. You just have to name it and it's all yours. *(LEO groans.)* Well. I'll be upstairs. When it gets really warm like this, I ... no, I can't tell you.

LEO. Oh tell me, please.

MEG. I can't.

LEO. Of course you can.

MEG. You won't tell anybody?

LEO. I promise. It'll be just between us girls.

MEG. Well... when it gets really warm, I like to take off all my clothes and sprinkle water on my chest and just lie down on the bed spread out like a flag! *(LEO gulps.)* Have you ever tried it?

LEO. I do it all the time.

MEG. I'll see you later.

(MEG runs up the stairs to the door on the balcony.)

LEO.Oh, Margaret.By the way, which room is mine and Stephanie's?

MEG. This one. Mine. We're all sharing. The three of us. Isn't that great?!

LEO... Great.

(MEG EXITS, closing the door. LEO buckles at the knees.)

LEO. Oh God. Now we're in trouble. Jack! Jack!... Stephanie!

(LEO dashes out through the garden. The instant he's gone, JACK and AUDREY enter through the doors to the hall.)

AUDREY. COME WITH ME. I'LL SHOW YOU WHERE YOUR BEDROOM IS.

(AUDREY leads JACK up the stairs.)

AUDREY. Now this is your bedroom. Sleep. Snore. ZZZZ. Okay? I'll see ya later. *(JACK hugs her.)* Aw... Bye-bye. Now go ahead. Into your room.

(JACK goes into the room and closes the door.)

    AUDREY. Gee, what a nice girl.

(She walks away.)

    JACK. *(Off.)* AHHHHHHHHH!!!
    MEG. *(Off.)* AHHHHHHHHHH!!!

(JACK reels out of the room and stumbles across the balcony. MEG hurries out of the room with a towel around her. LEO REEN-TERS from the garden at the same time.)

    JACK. Oh my God! Oh my God!
    MEG. Stephanie, it's all right!
    JACK. Oh my God!
    AUDREY. Wait! Wait! Meg, listen! Holy cow! Stephanie is talking!

(MEG gasps.)

    MEG. Maxine! Did you hear that. She's talking!

(LEO drops to his knees and throws his arms up to Heaven.)

    LEO. Oh thank God! It's a miracle!

(Religious music. Trumpets and organ. Blackout.)

END OF ACT ONE

ACT II

Scene 1

(The lights come up on the living room, late afternoon, three days later. FLORENCE is hurrying out the door of her downstairs bedroom, pursued by DOC, who has a stethoscope around his neck.)

DOC. Florence!

FLORENCE. Shut up!

DOC. Will you please stay in bed!

FLORENCE. No!

DOC. Florence, if you don't listen to me, you are going to die!

FLORENCE. How would you know?

DOC. Because I will strangle you to death.

FLORENCE. I want to see Stephanie! My baby is talking! Someone could have told me about it three days ago!

DOC. You were hardly breathing three days ago, you were on life support!

FLORENCE. Well I still had ears, didn't I?!! I could have listened! I could have nodded my head!!

(FLORENCE makes a break for the front door.)

DOC. Florence get back in that bed.

*(At which moment, JACK ENTERS dressed as STEPHANIE, in a
    day dress.)*

FLORENCE. Stephanie! Stephanie, there you are! I just heard
the news. Let me hear you speak.

JACK. *(At a loss; then, wispy and flower-like.)* ... I need a drink.

FLORENCE. Oh, my heart! Did you hear that? The tone. The
lightness. It's her mother's voice.

JACK. Dear Mama. So sweet. So gentle. When she entered the
room it was like a summer breeze.

FLORENCE. She weighed three hundred pounds.

JACK. Yes. Of course. But so light on her feet ...

FLORENCE. It's true, it's true! Now tell me, how does it feel,
speaking aloud for the first time? Is it exciting?

JACK. Well, it is quite a surprise in some ways. In my head, I
always sounded like Lucille Ball.

(DUNCAN ENTERS.)

DUNCAN. Well, good morning. Florence. Stephanie. I was looking for Margaret.

JACK. I believe that she and Maxine went shopping for the day.
In Philadelphia.

FLORENCE. Isn't it amazing, Duncan. Stephanie, talking after
all these years.

DUNCAN. Amazing. Almost miraculous.

JACK. But as a man of the cloth, surely you believe in miracles,
Reverend Wooley.

DUNCAN. Well, I believe that miracles happen to people who
are deserving of miracles.

JACK. And you don't think that I'm deserving?

DUNCAN. Well, you might be, but I don't know you very well, now do I? You came onto the scene somewhat unexpectedly. At a rather unfortunate time.

JACK. *(Starting to whimper, trying to hide the tears.)* Oh, dear, I'm sorry if I'm a nuisance...

DUNCAN. I didn't say that —

JACK. Perhaps Maxine and I should just go home ...

FLORENCE. Don't even think about it!

JACK. *(Weeping now.)* But he said that we're unfortunate!

DUNCAN. I didn't say that either!

FLORENCE. Duncan, be quiet!

JACK. But if he doesn't like us, then we should go.

FLORENCE. Oh, who cares what he thinks. I never liked him anyway.

DUNCAN. Florence!

FLORENCE. Stephanie, come to my room!

JACK. Actually, I thought I might take a walk ...

FLORENCE. To my room! Now!

JACK. Yes, Aunt Florence.

DOC. Florence, I'll be back tomorrow.

FLORENCE. Don't do me any favors, Dr. Crippen. Just stay away from me! Stephanie!

JACK. Coming!

(FLORENCE EXITS, followed by JACK.)

DOC. I don't understand it. She's getting stronger by the minute. It must have something to do with the rise of evil in the world, it's giving her strength.

DUNCAN. Doctor, don't you find it incredible that a woman who has been deaf and dumb all her life is suddenly talking like this?

DOC. Well, there have been cases like this before, medically speaking. Usually caused by some jolt to the system. Apparently in her case it was the shock of seeing Meg lying there on the bed, buck naked.

DUNCAN. Doctor —

DOC. Of course, that would do anybody a lot of good. If I'd been in her shoes I'd have done a lot more than start talking. Ha!

DUNCAN. Doctor, please!

DOC. Please what?! It's called living, Duncan. Sex. Living. Humor. Have you heard of these things?! I have to go. I have patients to see. I have a real job.

(When DOC is gone, DUNCAN looks around furtively, then he goes to the telephone and dials a number.)

DUNCAN. Hello? Inspector Ballard, please. ... Ah, good, it's Reverend Wooley. Now, have you made any progress concerning the two women? ... Yes, I know it's only been two days, but... No, I don't have any evidence. That's what I want you to find. ... No, I don't know that they're frauds. I suspect they are. ... Because they're odd! ... Well for one thing, they're very large women, and — ... Well yes, people do vary in size, but ...well one of them was deaf and dumb since birth and now she's talking! ... Well yes, I suppose I'm happy for her, but... Look, officer, I can't put my finger on it, but they're not being honest about something. They're sort of... shady. ... No, they haven't tried to get me in a card game! I don't play cards, I'm a minister!... Well... yes, bridge occasionally.

MEG. *(Off.)* Duncan?

DUNCAN. *(Quickly.)* Look, I have to go now, just keep working on it. I'll call you later. Good-bye.

(As DUNCAN hangs up, MEG hurries in carrying several purchases,

including a dress box. She's wearing a pretty new hat and a duster over her dress. She's in high spirits.)

MEG. Oh, Duncan, wait till you hear! Maxine and I had a day out together and we had the most wonderful time! First we went shopping at Saks Fifth Avenue!, and Maxine insisted I get this dress for the party. At first, in the dressing room, I couldn't even get it on. But then Maxine helped me into it. Poor thing. As she was pulling it over my hips, she got faint. Then we had lunch at the Bellevue and we ordered snails, then we had our nails done, then more shopping at this little boutique where they simply worship Maxine, then tea at the Ritz, at the corner table, and I had a champagne cocktail!

DUNCAN. Ah.

MEG. Is something wrong?

DUNCAN. No, no... I would have liked to have known you were going, that's all...

MEG. I'm sorry, Duncan. I forgot to tell you. But Maxine says it's so important to be spontaneous in life. Try new things, take chances. As they say in French, metmoyer!

(MEG removes her coat to reveal that she's wearing a stylish new dress.)

DUNCAN. Margaret!

MEG. Do you like it?

DUNCAN. It's a little snug, isn't it?

MEG. Maybe a little... But listen, I have something to tell you. We went to a bridal shop and looked at wedding gowns.

DUNCAN. Margaret! We agreed on business attire!

MEG. I know. She just wanted me to look. But she says that a bride should have a gown. And an engagement ring. She says it means so much to a girl.

DUNCAN. Well, heh heh, not all girls would agree with her there. Mm? Right?

MEG. Well, I do think a ring would be nice, Duncan.

DUNCAN. You do?

MEG. Yes. I do.

DUNCAN. *(Nettled.)* Well why didn't you say so before?

MEG. I did but you weren't listening.

DUNCAN. No you didn't.

MEG. Yes I did.

DUNCAN. You did not!

MEG. Do we have to argue about it?

DUNCAN. We are not arguing! If you want a ring, you can have a ring. I just want to make you happy. You know that.

MEG. Maxine says that you have to pick it.

DUNCAN. Of course I'll pick it.

MEG. She says it should have a diamond in the middle.

DUNCAN. Fine, I'll get a diamond.

MEG. With a platinum setting.

DUNCAN. Who is this for?! You or Maxine?!

MEG. Duncan, you're yelling at me.

DUNCAN. No I'm not! It's just... I have been under a great deal of strain. Now if you'll excuse me, I have some charity work to do.

(DUNCAN leaves. MEG passes a mirror and notices herself. She poses, admiring herself in her new dress. LEO appears at the garden doors, dressed as a man, but she doesn't see him. He looks every inch the star actor. MEG strikes another pose, more daring. She notices how the dress emphasizes her breasts — she has cleavage! — and she starts to shimmy in front of the mirror, like a stripper, really going way out on a limb. As she gyrates in front of the mirror, LEO walks further into the room and watches

... and then she sees him.)

MEG. Yahhh!

LEO. Excuse me. Sorry. Is this the home of a Miss Florence Snider?

(MEG recognizes him immediately as "LEO CLARK" and gasps.)

MEG... Yes, it is.

LEO. Oh, good. I'm looking for someone who's staying here —

MEG. Maxine.

LEO. That's right. How do you ...?

MEG. You're Leo Clark, aren't you?!

LEO. *(Puzzled.)* Yes.

MEG. *(Curtsying instinctively, overcome with awe.)* Oh, how do you do! Please, come in. I'm Maxine's cousin. Meg. And I am just so thrilled to meet you! Maxine has told me all about you. Which I knew already! Because of who you are. I mean, Leo Clark. ... She'll be along in a minute. We just got back from a little shopping spree. She had something to do at the station. Well. She had to use the bathroom, but I suppose I shouldn't say that. *(She laughs nervously.)* Would you like to sit down?

LEO. I'm fine.

MEG. I just want to say how... kind it is of you to come all this way. And I am so thrilled about being in a play with you... and-and if you want to back out of it, I understand. I mean, you're an actor. A real actor. You have a body. ... I mean, your body is trained. It's an instrument. A treasure. And my treasure isn't trained at all. My instrument. My body! The way yours is.

(She looks away and makes a face. She wants to kill herself.)

LEO. *(Quietly.)* You have the most beautiful eyes I have ever seen. I'll go find Maxine.

(LEO EXITS through the garden. MEG is in a daze. Then JACK, still dressed as STEPHANIE, ENTERS from the hall.)

JACK. Margaret? ... Did you have a nice outing? Are you all right?

MEG. Oh, Stephanie. I just met the most intriguing man.

(Without warning, LEO reenters.)

LEO. Sorry, just one more thing ...

JACK. AHH!

MEG. Stephanie, this is Leo Clark. The famous actor!

JACK. You-you-you-

MEG. She's speechless. I know just how she feels. Stephanie is Maxine's sister. Have you two met before?

LEO. No, but she's even prettier than Maxine said she was. Anyway, I just wanted to say that rehearsal starts tomorrow at ten.

MEG. I wouldn't miss it for the world. *(To Jack.)* We're putting on a play at the wedding.

JACK. Oh, really? Well, that's news to me.

MEG. Maxine is directing and Mr. Clark and I are starring in it! Wait. Do you think that Stephanie could be in it?

LEO. Well, I suppose we could put her in the dance at the end. Like some enormous elf or sprite...

MEG. Oh, that's wonderful. Isn't he wonderful?

JACK. Mmmmm...

MEG. Wait! There are some lines I need to ask you about. For the play. I marked them in my copy and it's in my room someplace. I'll be right back. Don't go way. All right?

LEO. Of course.

(She backs away, trying to be sophisticated, and trips on her packages. Then she gathers them all up and runs off. But she's gone out through the wrong door — and she hurries right back in to the room.)

MEG. The, uh, bedroom's upstairs ...

(She fumbles her way up the stairs and into her bedroom, closing the door with a bang. JACK turns, furious.)

JACK. You crumb.
LEO. I can explain —
JACK. You traitor.
LEO. I did it for both of us.
JACK. You did not! You did it to get Meg! So you could just-just-just-

(He indicates sexual intercourse.)

LEO. Jack!
JACK. You have put my entire life in jeopardy so you could have a little snog in the grass!
LEO. That's not true!
JACK. You want to play the hero and wear trousers and fool around, while I have to wear this stinking dress and this GODDAM BRASSIERE!
LEO. Would you keep it down!
JACK. NO! Hey! Where are you going?!
LEO. *(Exiting.)* Any place until you keep your voice down.
JACK. Get back here, I'm not finished! ... Leo! Get back in

here or you can go to hello ...! *(As LEO runs out, DUNCAN EN-TERS — so JACK has to immediately turn his galloping man-walk into a mincing female-walk.)* Ta-ta, good-bye.

(JACK EXITS, and DUNCAN strides into the room, simply ecstatic.)

DUNCAN. Meg! Meg?! Meg, get down here!

(MEG ENTERS from above.)

MEG. Duncan, what is it? Where's Mr. Clark?
DUNCAN. Who?
MEG. Leo Clark, the actor. He was just here.
DUNCAN. Fine, fine, fine, now listen. I was walking past the house just now and one of those Western Union boys was coming to the door. I said can I help you, he said do you live here and I said yes —
MEG. But you don't live here.
DUNCAN. I know that. That's not the point! He brought this telegram addressed to you. I gave him a tip by the way, so you might want to re-im... no, forget it. But listen to this!
MEG. Duncan —
DUNCAN. Just listen! "Saw advertisement in London Times. Stop. Both of us thrilled. Stop. Embarking from Southampton tomorrow and will arrive your house morning of June 8. Stop. Love, Maxine and Stephanie!" Ha, ha! Ha, ha, ha, ha, ha, ha!
MEG. *(Taking the telegram.)* I don't understand.
DUNCAN. Understand what? It's obvious. These two are your real cousins! They arrive here the day before the wedding. And so the ones who came on Monday, those horrible, big, pushy creatures, are both frauds. Hee, hee, hee, hee, hee, hee! I knew it! Oh, it'll be just like old times. *(With a Russian accent:)* "Dahnce vit me, my

dahlink."

(He dances her around the room.)

MEG. Duncan, stop it! This is ridiculous!

(He gives her a big kiss on the lips. The news has made him passionate. When the kiss breaks off, she keeps talking as though nothing has happened.)

MEG. Maxine is wonderful. And so is Stephanie. They can't be frauds.

DUNCAN. Margaret, they are not your cousins. They have come here to fool you and take your money.

MEG. I don't believe you.

DUNCAN. Well then how do you explain this telegram? Huh? "Love, Maxine and Stephanie!"

MEG. Well... I suppose that... wait. It's simple. They must be the frauds. That's it, I'm sure of it!

DUNCAN. Oh, Margaret —

MEG. They have to be, and I'll tell you why. I can prove it. Because Maxine — our Maxine, the real one — knows Leo Clark, the famous actor, and they're old friends! She even asked him here and he just arrived!

DUNCAN. So what? That doesn't prove anything!

MEG. Of course it does! He's an established actor, everyone knows him, and she's one of his best friends!

DUNCAN. Well maybe this best friend of his is a con artist.

MEG. Oh, stop it.

DUNCAN. And maybe he's in on it, too! Have you thought of that?! They could be splitting the boodle!

MEG. Oh, Duncan. He's Leo Clark. He's in the theatre. Theatre people wouldn't do that kind of thing!

DUNCAN. Wouldn't d - !! Meg, they are actors, they lie for a living! That's their profession! They are all big liars!! Look, look, look, we can decide this easily, right now, no problem. We will show your so-called friends this telegram, you will stand here and watch their reactions and that will settle it, case closed.

MEG. Duncan. You will not show them that telegram. Ever.

DUNCAN. What?

MEG. I will not have them offended in this house.

DUNCAN. But Marg —

MEG. They are the sweetest, kindest women that ever lived and I will not let you do it.

DUNCAN. But they are not your cousins!

MEG. Yes they are! And if you tell them a single word about that telegram — just one word — I'll-I'll-I'll do something. And that's final! Especially now that Leo Clark is here.

DUNCAN. "Leo Clark." What is he doing here anyway?

(Beat. MEG takes a breath. Her heart is pounding, but she tries to look unfazed.)

MEG. He's starring in a play... which we're putting on the night before the wedding... which I will be playing in as well... as an actress. So now you know.

DUNCAN. Margaret!

MEG. I'm sorry, Duncan, but that's how it is. Now please go. I have to study my lines. I'll see you later.

(DUNCAN tries to say something, but he's speechless. He turns and leaves with as much dignity as he can muster. MEG has never stood up for herself like this before and it's been the ordeal of a lifetime. When DUNCAN is gone, she takes a deep breath to

*calm herself. Then she snatches up her copy of the play and
bounds to the French doors.)*

MEG. *(At the doors; romantically, as Viola in Twelfth Night.)* O
time, thou must untangle this, not I / It is too hard a knot for me
t'untie.

*(With a look of determination, she hurries out of the room — as the
scene changes to:)*

Scene 2

*(The living room, ten days later, mid-morning. DOC ENTERS in his
Elizabethan costume for the play, as Sir Toby Belch, including
scarlet tights, a doublet, a sword, and an impressive codpiece.)*

DOC. Butch, come on!
BUTCH. *(Off.)* No!
DOC. Butch now stop it! The rehearsal starts in two minutes!
BUTCH. *(Off.)* I'm not coming out!
DOC. Butch, I'm telling you, it's a nice costume. You look ter-
rific. Now get out here!

*(BUTCH ENTERS dressed as Sir Andrew Aguecheek. He wears
baggy hose, a moth-eaten doublet and a floppy hat from which
emerges a wig of straight blond hair that looks like yellow straw
sticking out to his shoulders.)*

BUTCH. I look like a broom with shoes on.

(AUDREY ENTERS in costume. She's dressed as Sebastian, an Elizabethan man.)

AUDREY. Good morning, everybody!

DOC & BUTCH. Morning!/Morning!

AUDREY. *(Striking a pose.)* "This is the air; that is the glorious sun;

(JACK ENTERS dressed as STEPHANIE — but not in costume for Twelfth Night.)

JACK. Good morning!

AUDREY. This pearl she gave me, I do feel't and see't ..."

BUTCH. "En garde! Ha! Ha! Ha!... Ha! Ha!

DOC. "What a plague means my niece to take the death of her brother thus."

JACK. "Item, two lips indifferent red; item, two grey eyes with lids to them —"

(LEO ENTERS, as LEO, carrying his script.)

LEO. Good morning, everyone. *("Morning/Morning.")* It's time for rehearsal. Let's get started. Sofa, please.

(Everyone pitches in to move the furniture out of the way.)

JACK. *(To AUDREY.)* Oh, isn't this fun! I just love rehearsals. Here, give us a hug.

AUDREY. Aww ...

JACK. Give us another.

AUDREY. Aww ...

JACK. Give us a — *(LEO coughs pointedly.)* Oh, sorry.
LEO. Right. Sit down, sit down.

(MEG ENTERS dressed as Viola/Caesario — and so her costume is identical to AUDREY's. It's a glorious costume with mirrored patchwork and rakish hat with a feather.)

MEG. Hi everyone, I'm sorry I'm late.

(She and AUDREY see each other — and realizing that they look identical, scream for joy, then strike a mirror-image pose.)

LEO. One face, one voice, one habit and two persons; / A natural perspective, that is, and is not. Sit down, please. *(Everyone sits on the floor facing LEO.)* Now Maxine, our esteemed director, has asked me to give you a few notes while she's out looking for props.
JACK. I thought she did that yesterday.
LEO. She's doing it again.
JACK. Oh. She does that quite a lot, doesn't she?
LEO. Well, Stephanie, there are a lot of props in the play.
JACK. And therefore she just disappears.
LEO. Exactly.
JACK. Aha. That's very informative. Thank you, Leo, you good-looking hunk of man, you.
LEO. Thank you, Stephanie. Now Meg, I want to... *(STEPHANIE raises her hand.)* Yes, Stephanie?
JACK. May I be excused? I have to use the little ladies.
LEO. Please do.
JACK. Thank you. I'll be back in a moment. *(To AUDREY)* Give us a hug. Ta ta.

(JACK EXITS.)

LEO. Now Meg we'll start with you. A general note, remember to keep your head up so we can see your face.

MEG. Right.

LEO. And I want you to articulate every word. "My father had a daughter." Try it.

(MEG stands, takes a breath; then does the Viola speech from Act 2, Scene 4 — and does it beautifully.)

MEG. "My father had a daughter loved a man — As it might be perhaps, were I a woman, I should your lordship."

LEO. *(As Orsino.)* "And what's her history?"

MEG. "A blank, my lord. She never told her love,
  But let concealment, like a worm in the bud,
  Feed on her damask cheek. She pined in thought,
  And with a green and yellow melancholy,
  She sat like Patience on a monument,
  Smiling at grief. Was not this love indeed?"

LEO. Much better. Just keep practicing. Tongue, tongue. "Was not this love indeed."

MEG. *(With her own meaning.)* "Was not this love indeed."

(She sits.)

LEO. Good. Doctor. Because you're doubling as the Sea Captain and Sir Toby, you might want to create a different physical presence for each one. Perhaps, as the Captain, you might stoop a little. The old sea dog type. Then as Sir Toby, you might be more ... rollicking.

DOC. Rollicking. Got it.

LEO. Butch.

BUTCH. Yes sir!

LEO. Don't rush your lines so much.

BUTCH. I can't help it. I get nervous.

LEO. Try it for me.

BUTCH. Now? In front of everybody?

LEO. Butch, in ten days, you'll be doing it in front of a hundred people. Stand up.

(BUTCH groans. He stands up and poses stiffly.)

LEO. Now just relax. *(LEO does a relaxing exercise, shaking his arms and humming. BUTCH imitates it. BUTCH then does each of the things that LEO now suggests:)* Bend your knees a little. Now let your arms hang at your sides. Look up. And relax your jaw. *(By this time, BUTCH looks like a gargoyle with rickets.)* We'll get there.

(At which moment, JACK ENTERS through the garden, dressed as himself.)

JACK. Knock knock? Leo! It's me! Jack! *(LEO is shocked. How did JACK do that so fast? Perhaps he screams as JACK did when LEO first appeared as LEO in the previous scene.)* Your friend, Jack! I heard you were in these parts, so I thought I'd drop by.

AUDREY. Oh my gosh. Hey, remember me? We met on the train!

JACK. Audrey.

MEG. Hello, I'm Meg. I saw you in Philadelphia -

BUTCH. My name's Butch!

AUDREY. I was wondering if I'd see you again...

DOC. Hi, I'm Doctor Myers...

LEO. Excuse me. Excuse me! ... We're having a rehearsal.

THE ACTORS. Sorry... sorry...

(They retreat to their seats on the floor.)

LEO. For those of you who don't know him this is Jack Gable, who used to be an old friend of mine.

(The following exchange is one of utterly false bonhomie.)

JACK. Are you surprised to see me? Huh? Just a little?

LEO. No, I've been expecting you for quite some time. I was simply waiting for you to think of it.

JACK. Well, when I heard that you had arrived here, I thought "Now why should he have all the fun?"

LEO. Because I thought of it first and I have a real reason for being here. Ha.

JACK. Ha, ha.

LEO. Ha, ha, ha.

JACK. Ha ha ha ha.

BOTH. Hahahahahahahahahaha.

(The cast joins in the fun.)

LEO. Now please sit down, we're rehearsing.

JACK. Right.

(JACK and AUDREY sit next to each other, quite cozy together.)

LEO. All right. Butch. Your lines. And don't rush.

BUTCH. "Sir-Toby-Belch-how-now-Sir Toby! I'll-stay-a-month-longer-I-am-a-fellow-of-the-strangest-mind-in-the-world-I-delight-in- masques-and-revels-sometimes-altogether-and-I-excel-at-kikshaws-of-every-kind-and-I-think-I-have-the-back-trick-

LEO. Stop, stop, STOP! THAT'S TOO FAST! *(BUTCH turns away, hurt.)* No. I'm sorry. I-I shouldn't have yelled. I'm sorry.

JACK. You know, I think Maxine could help right now. She listens better than you do.

LEO. Surprisingly, that's a good idea. I'll go find her. Everybody, take five.

(LEO EXITS. The actors relax and start chatting. BUTCH is low.)

BUTCH. Gee, I'm tryin' to slow down. I really am.

JACK. You'll be fine, I promise. Look. Try this. After every, say, five words, take a breath and say to yourself the word ... Mississippi.

BUTCH. I can do that!

DOC. Of course you can! You could be a star! It just takes practice.

BUTCH. Thanks, Dad. And you're doing great!

DOC. Aw. Come on. As they say in show biz, let's "run your lines."

(They move away, leaving AUDREY and JACK alone together.)

AUDREY. Hey. You're really nice, ya know that?

JACK. You know what? The feeling is mutual.

AUDREY. Aw, get outa here... So what brings you to York, PA?

JACK. The truth? I've been having dreams about roller skating and I thought of you.

AUDREY. Gee that's nice.

JACK. How's the play coming?

AUDREY. It's coming great. But the thing is, I'm playing somebody of the opposite sex. His name is Sebastian. He's supposed to be Meg's twin brother, which is nuts. Me as a guy! But I've thought up an angle. See, I'm gonna play him as a real tough guy. I do this great Marlon Brando imitation, but I figure I won't tell Maxine till later. I'll just surprise her.

JACK. What a good idea.

AUDREY. So how do you know Maxine and Stephanie?

JACK. Me? Oh, they... didn't they tell you? Well, they-they practically raised me.

AUDREY. No kiddin'.

JACK. I can still remember Stephanie singing me to sleep every night.

AUDREY. But I thought she was deaf and dumb till recently.

JACK. She used a tape recorder and moved her lips.

AUDREY. Are you puttin' me on? Get outa here.

JACK. Here, give us a hug... I mean, me a hug. Give me a hug.

(AUDREY hugs him, slightly confused. At this moment, LEO ENTERS from the hall, dressed as MAXINE in a very chic pants outfit, having changed in a hurry. She's in director mode now, flying everywhere, half business, half Bernhardt.)

LEO. Darlings! Oh, my darlings, forgive me! *(Into the garden.)* Thank you, Leo! Take your time! I was scouting for props amid the roiling sea of the York County merchants. Jack! Jack! My dear boy!

JACK. Maxine! How good to see you!

LEO. Oh let me look at you. Why, you've put on weight. You're getting enormously fat.

JACK. Well you look marvelous. You've always had that big, raw-boned mannish look.

LEO. Why thank you. Aren't you sweet. *(He pinches JACK's cheek and has to restrain himself from doing JACK an injury.)* Now Jack dear, do me a favor and go find Stephanie. I need her for rehearsal. And tell her to get into costume.

LEADING LADIES

JACK. Costume? Now?

LEO. Yes now, dear, before anyone gets hurt.

JACK. Oh all right.

(JACK EXITS.)

LEO. Now let's all take another minute while I settle down. Chat among yourselves. Whoo. Hot. I'm afraid I rushed too much...

(She blows down into her blouse, and she sits next to MEG.)

LEO. So. My dear. How is it coming along? Do you feel bright-eyed and bushy-tailed?

MEG. *(Troubled.)* Well, it's coming, I guess. But not the way I hoped it would.

LEO. Is something wrong?

MEG. Well, not really.

LEO. "Well not really." That doesn't sound very promising at all. Can you tell me about it?

MEG. Well, it's just... I've never done any real acting before and there's so much to remember. Head up. Enunciate. Move left, move right. You and Leo are professionals. And you work with professionals. From the Royal Academy! And they're all sophisticated, and they know everything and they've been everywhere. ... I just... I can't imagine what Leo must think of me.

(She's ready to cry by this time.)

LEO. Margaret. *(He takes her hand.)* Let me tell you something. I'll say it once, and I don't want to say it again. You are an extraordinary woman. You can do anything you set your mind to. And everyone has to start some place. Olivier was born in some dinky little town in Southern England, and Katherine Hepburn was born in Cape Cod someplace with a knife in her teeth. You are not defined by where you start, but by where you end up. As for the play, there are two rules for every actor: remember your lines and don't bump into the furniture. That is my line. Noel Coward stole it from me. As for traveling or not traveling, you will get to Paris one of these days if I have to carry you on my back and swim. And when you get there, you will look around and say to yourself: I was just as sophisticated before I left, only now I need a bath. All right?

MEG... All right.

LEO. Good. And remember: Lines,

MEG. And furniture. Got it. Maxine... thank you for staying for the wedding.

LEO. My dear, I think of nothing else.

(At this moment, JACK REENTERS as STEPHANIE, only he's dressed for his role as OLIVIA in something wildly seductive and outrageous — Spanish perhaps — and he's not happy about it.)

JACK. Well. Are you happy now?

LEO. Stephanie. You look as ridi - as charming as I hoped you would. All right, everyone, line up, please. Line up. Let me see my cast all together. Let's go ...

(The cast lines up, a truly motley crew of all shapes and sizes, variously terrified [BUTCH], over-confident [DOC], confused [AUDREY], annoyed [JACK] and thrilled [MEG]. They should remind us of the mechanicals in A Midsummer Night's Dream — a valiant band of well-meaning locals who haven't got a clue.)

LEO. Now I want each of you to recite your favorite line from

the play, in character, reaching way down deep, showing me the
absolute finest performance of which you are capable. Sir Toby.

*(Each character steps forward, does his or her speech and steps
back in line.)*

SIR TOBY/DOC. *(Rollicking, hands on hips — truly awful.)*
What a plague means my niece to take the death of her brother thus?!
Ha! Ha! I'm sure care's an enemy to life! Ha ha! Ho ho! Ha ha!
Rollicking.

SIR ANDREW/BUTCH. *(Strikes his pose.)*
Methinks sometimes
I have no more wit, Mississippi,
Than a Christian or an ordinary man has, Mississippi!
Oh had I but followed the arts, Mississippi!

OLIVIA/JACK. *(The great diva.)*
By the roses of the spring,
By maidenhood, honor, truth and everything,
I love thee so, in spite of all thy pride,
Nor wit nor reason can my passion hide!

VIOLA/MEG.
As I am man,
My state is desperate for my master's love.
As I am woman *(Now alas the day!)*,
What thriftless sighs shall poor Olivia breathe?

SEBASTIAN/AUDREY. *(Very Brando, both in voice and ges-
ture.)*
Ah, me. My stars shine darkly over me.
I seek in this strange land my sister,
My twin, in hope she is not drowned.

LEO. And there you have it. Each one better than the next.
Soon this room will be decorated like a fairy land and we, the actors

of this comedy called life, will be presenting a one-in-a-million performance of Twelfth Night, and all I can say is May God Be With
Us!

(The lights change and the cast scatters.)

Scene 3

*(As the lights change, we hear a dance band in the garden playing a
popular dance tune of the period over the clinking of party
glasses. In a blue half-light, our company of actors helps move
the furniture back into place; simultaneously, stagehands dressed
as caterers begin decorating the room with flowers, a screen
and a punch bowl and glasses. Small white fairy lights come on
in the garden – and by the end of the transition, the room looks
joyfully party-like.*
*It's ten days later and the party is in progress. Just as the caterers
finish decorating the room, the lights come up on the balcony
above the living room, and DUNCAN enters from down the hall.
There's a telephone up there, outside Meg's bedroom, and he
picks up the receiver and dials, furtively. He's extremely upset.)*

FLORENCE. *(Off.)* Duncan, get down here!
DUNCAN. *(Calling.)* I'll be down in a minute, Florence! *(To
himself.)* You old bat! *(Into the phone.)* Ah, Inspector Ballard, it's
Reverend Wooley again. Sorry to bother you at this...Yes, I know
it's seven-thirty, but I've been trying to get you all ...Well, you didn't
answer any of the messages! Now listen, I'm at Florence's house
right now, at the party. ...Well I'm sorry you weren't invited but I

wasn't in charge of the guest list. ...Well, yes, I had some influence, but...Yes, the food is excellent, I'm very sorry you weren't invited, but please just listen! Do you remember I told you about the telegram from the real Maxine and Stephanie — well, it said they'd arrive this morning and they aren't here yet! Of course it has me worried! I told you about this whole thing weeks ago! You were supposed to help me! Yes I am, very upset, and I'll tell you why. Because Maxine, the big one, told me this morning that she overheard Florence changing her will. She's leaving everything to Stephanie, the smaller one. ... Yes, they're both large, but one is bigger than the other! The point is, Stephanie doesn't deserve it! ... Well, yes, I hope Florence lasts forever, but it isn't very likely, now is it!?

FLORENCE. *(Off.)* Duncan!

DUNCAN. Shut up! *(Into the phone.)* All right, I'll tell you what I think you should do. I think you should arrest them both. Right now. Send a squad car. ... Of course you need evidence, but you were supposed to find it! That's your job! ... I'm not criticizing you! I'm stating a fact!

FLORENCE. *(Off.)* Duncan! Where the hell are you?!

DUNCAN. I'M COMING! *(Into the phone, desperate.)* Look, just do something, but do it now! ... Thank you! *(He hangs up.)* God!

(He realizes what he just said — at which moment, the lights change and a tango starts to play. FLORENCE appears, dressed to the nines, and starts tangoing. She has taken years of lessons and has great flair. DUNCAN ENTERS and joins her. He's miserable. They complete the first section of the dance and dance out — as AUDREY and BUTCH dance into the room. AUDREY is terrific, BUTCH is trying hard to keep up. They perform the second section and then go — as STEPHANIE and DOC enter

tangoing up a storm. Shades of "Some Like It Hot." When they complete the third section, the other couples come back on and all three couples dance the coda in unison and end with a flourish. Note: this should be choreographed as a real dance number. When the dance is over, everyone filters off into the garden, except FLORENCE and AUDREY, who linger for a moment.)

AUDREY. Ooh, this is such a good party, I can tell already. And just wait'll you see the play tonight. You'll go insane.

FLORENCE. Well, that's something to look forward to.

AUDREY. You know, I've just gotta say, it's really nice of you to do this for Meg. Next time somebody says to me you're nothin' but a nasty old bat, I'm gonna say, "Oh yeah? You only know the half of it."

FLORENCE. Thank you.

(As they EXIT, LEO and JACK ENTER simultaneously, JACK from the garden. LEO is LEO, dressed in a dinner jacket, and JACK is Stephanie, in a party dress, just having danced.)

LEO. Jack — !

JACK. If I have to dance one more minute in high heels, I'll kill myself. You should see them out there, hip, sway, hip, sway. I'm telling you it's a whole other sex.

LEO. Jack listen! We have to stop the wedding.

JACK. Stop the — ... Why? What are you talking about?!

LEO. So that I can marry Meg.

JACK. Marry her? I thought you just wanted to ...

(He indicates sexual intercourse.)

LEO. Jack, I'm in love with her!

LEADING LADIES

JACK. Oh, really? So you've been stringing me along the whole time under false pretenses! And what about Julius Caesar?! Huh?! And-and-and King Lear, and Hamlet! That's what you live for!

LEO. Yes. I did. And I want all that. If it's possible. But Jack, I'm in love. Deeply in love. I want a house, and neighbors and a front door.

JACK. That was my idea!

LEO. And you were right! You were exactly right! And we're almost there. It could be us.

JACK. "Us?" What have I got to do with this?

LEO. Well you and Audrey.

JACK. What do you mean?! We're ... friends.

LEO. Jack, whenever she walks into the room, you start drooling. And last night she told me she's in love with you. She wants to marry you.

JACK. ... She said that? *(LEO nods. JACK is speechless, then he explodes with joy.)* Hoo-hooooo! Ha-haaaaaaaa! Yes!!! Yyyyyyyyyyes!!! I knew it! Ha-haaaaaaaa!

Did she really say that?

LEO. No, but you can see the effect it has on you.

JACK. Leo —!

LEO. Now listen. Jack. You've got to help me. I have spent three weeks trying to convince Meg to leave Duncan and marry me and I've gotten nowhere. She feels obligated to him. So, I have a plan. The final gambit. I want you to seduce Duncan. Offer him your body. As Stephanie, of course.

JACK. What?

LEO. You see, this morning I told Duncan that I overheard Florence talking to her lawyer, cutting Margaret and Maxine out of her will and leaving everything to Stephanie. Well Duncan is beside himself! He wants the money for some foundation or something. So if you give him even the slightest encouragement he'll go after you. Now here's the trick: Meg and I will be hiding behind this screen watching everything. We'll jump out and catch him the second he starts to undress you.

JACK. Un-un-undress -

LEO. It's the old screen gambit, like in Twelfth Night and School for Scandal.

JACK. Are you crazy? ARE YOU NUTS?!!!!!

LEO. Jack! You have to do this. When Meg sees him for what he is, she'll give him up! Then I can marry her!

JACK. No.

LEO. Please.

JACK. No!

LEO. Jack, you're my best friend! If I ever needed you in my whole life, I need you now!

JACK. I have spent the last four weeks of my life dressed as a woman, I can't take a bath without you guarding the door, and I have nightmares, really horrible nightmares, about talking brassieres!

LEO. Is that a yes?

JACK. *(Whimpering.)* Yes.

LEO. Good. Here's the letter.

JACK. What letter?

LEO. From you to Duncan. *(Points to the envelope.)* See? "Duncan." It says that you'll meet him here at 8 o'clock and that you find him sexually attractive.

JACK. Oh, God!

(AUDREY ENTERS from the garden.)

AUDREY. Has anyone seen Jack?

JACK. Yes? *(Catches himself.)* No! No Jack. Not here. All gone.

LEO. Stephanie, you can ask her now.

JACK. Huh?

LEO. She's so shy. She wants you to deliver this letter.
AUDREY. Sure, no problem.

(She takes the envelope – as MEG enters at the top of the stairs dressed for the party and looking gorgeous. We hear a romantic song of the period wafting in from the garden.)

MEG. Hi everybody. Sorry to interrupt. Has anyone seen Duncan?
LEO. Duncan, Duncan, never heard of him. They're playing our song. Shall we dance?
MEG. Well... all right.

(They dance around the room like Fred Astaire and Ginger Rogers — then sweep out into the garden, leaving AUDREY and JACK alone. AUDREY sighs.)

AUDREY. Isn't love great. Some day I'm gonna find just the right guy. And believe you me, on that wedding night, in some big soft comfy bed, I'm gonna make him really happy. Hey, come here, you're drooling. *(She pulls out a hankie and mops around his mouth.)* Aw. Here. Give us a hug. Ooh! Stephanie, watch your fingers!
JACK. Sorry, sorry... I-I-I-I think I should go now. Bye-bye.

(He reels up the stairs and through the door.)

AUDREY. Gee she's a nice girl.

(AUDREY turns and accidentally drops the envelope in the punch bowl. She fishes it out and wipes it with her sleeve.)

AUDREY. Ahh! Oh, darn! Would you look at this envelope?

I'm supposed to deliver it and now I can't read it. Let's see... D. It starts with a D. D-U. Or is that an O? Who do I know that starts with a D ...? *(DOC ENTERS.)* Hi, Doc. ...... Wait! Doc. "D." Doctor. Doc, this letter is for you. It's from Stephanie.

DOC. For me?

AUDREY. She asked me to give it to you. See you later.

(And AUDREY EXITS. DOC is alone.)

DOC. From Stephanie? That's odd. *(He opens the letter and reads.)* "My dear friend, You are a healer of souls. You are a man of compassion to those in your care. You are my sunshine, my only sunshine, You make me happy when skies are gray... As the song says, I adore you." ... What? "As you know, I am now an heiress, but please don't let my millions stand in your way. I never felt religious until I met you, but now I want to sit on your pulpit. May you enter my house and dwell there forever." The woman is an animal! A very large animal! "Take me. Ravish me. Meet me tonight in the living room at 8 o'clock." That's in ten minutes! "Your loving and devoted, Stephanie. P.S. Don't take no for an answer." God in Heaven. She's just been playing hard to get! I should have known from that first time we met. She just looked at me and never said a word. Of course, she was deaf and dumb at the time. But still. She had those bedroom eyes. Droopy. Sensuous. Astigmatic. I shall return.

(He hurries out, as MEG and LEO dance in.)

MEG. Well. I can't believe it's finally happening. The wedding, I mean. I've actually been remarkably calm about it. Up to now. I don't know why, I guess it seemed so far away. But then suddenly, last night, as I was lying there in bed, my stomach got very tight, and my heart started—

(He stops her mouth with a kiss. A really great kiss.)

MEG. No!

LEO. Meg. I love you.

MEG. Leo, stop.

LEO. I can't. I love you more than anything in the world.

MEG. I'm getting married tomorrow!

LEO. Then don't. Not to him. Marry me instead.

MEG. Leo, I can't do that! I promised Duncan!

LEO. But he's not right for you! Meg, you deserve a life! You have to see Paris, and do some acting and travel the world! Now I have a plan, so just listen. You and I are going to stand right here, behind this screen and watch Duncan try to make lo —

MEG. I've got to go.

LEO. Not yet.

MEG. I need Maxine! I have to talk to her!

LEO. Maxine?!

MEG. I have to find her right now!

LEO. Oh no. No no. No no. No no. Wait!

(Too late. MEG is gone. As LEO runs after her, DUNCAN ENTERS jovially, carrying a telegram.)

DUNCAN. Why hello there, Leo.

LEO. You're early. Go away and come back.

(LEO runs out to the garden, following MEG, leaving DUNCAN alone in the room. DUNCAN is in high spirits.)

DUNCAN. "Go away and come back." Ha! I knew I was right.

Why look at this. It's another telegram — and it just arrived. *(He kisses the telegram with a big smack. "Mwa!")* "Apologize for delay. Stop. General strike at fault. Stop. Will arrive at eight fifteen tonight. Stop. Maxine and Stephanie." Ha! Ha! Ha! Oh, Justice is sweet, sayeth the Lord, hallelujah!

(JACK now ENTERS from the bedroom at the top of the stairs, still in his party gown, looking as sexy as all get out. He sees DUNCAN, kicks the door shut and drapes himself along the doorframe.)

JACK. ... Hello, big boy.

DUNCAN. I beg your pardon.

JACK. Is that a chopstick in your pocket or are you just glad to see me?

DUNCAN. Are you speaking to me?

JACK. Oh, yes.

DUNCAN. Well don't bother.

JACK. Fine, fine. No words, just action, is that your game? Well go ahead, mister! I'm ready for you! *(He poses with his dress hiked up above his knee. When DUNCAN isn't looking, he gives a high sign to the screen, believing that LEO is behind it. DUNCAN turns and just stares at him.)* What's the matter?

DUNCAN. The matter? Nothing's the matter for me. No-o-o. But it is for you. I have a surprise.

JACK. Here it comes.

DUNCAN. A big surprise.

JACK. Now you're just bragging.

DUNCAN. In fact, I have two surprises.

JACK. You have two of them?

DUNCAN. That's right. And they have long flowing hair.

JACK. Have you thought about surgery?

DUNCAN. Don't change the subject!

(JACK covers his eyes with his hand and keeps them covered throughout the following:)

JACK. All right. Go ahead.

DUNCAN. You want to see it, eh? *(DUNCAN goes through his pockets, looking for the telegram.)* Wait a second... I'll get it out... Oh, damn, now I can't find it ...

JACK. You can't find it?

DUNCAN. Just give me a second ...

JACK. And you call this a big surprise?

DUNCAN. Here it is. I found it. *(He pulls out the telegram and holds it up. But JACK is still hiding his eyes.)* There. Do you see it?

JACK. No.

DUNCAN. You're not looking.

JACK. I can't.

DUNCAN. At least look at the signature.

JACK. It's signed?

DUNCAN. Of course it's signed! How else would you know where it came from?!

(BING BONG! The front doorbell rings.)

DUNCAN. It's them. I know it is. Ha! Here! Keep it as a souvenir!

JACK. A souvenir ...?

(DUNCAN stuffs the telegram into JACK's hand and EXITS. JACK hurries over to the screen to talk to LEO — who isn't there, of course — when DOC ENTERS. JACK puts the telegram into his sleeve and forgets about it.)

DOC. Hello, gorgeous.

JACK. Ah! Oh, Doctor, thank God it's you. I just had the most awful experience!

DOC. Oh, you poor thing. You poor baby. You're upset, I can tell. Now you just sit down. Just tell your doctor aaaaall about it.

(DOC starts making love to JACK, stroking his hair and cheek.)

JACK. ... What are you doing?

DOC. Am I doing something?

JACK. Yes, now stop it.

DOC. Stop it, she says. Stop it. Ha! Can I have a kiss?

JACK. No!

DOC. Ouch! Give me that hand! Oh, you have such interesting hands. For the record, I do electrolysis.

(DOC really goes after STEPHANIE, who wriggles away and starts crawling across the floor.)

JACK. Hey! Would you stop that! Stop it! Just-just-just- That's personal property!

DOC. Who said "Don't take no for an answer?"

JACK. I have no idea.

DOC. "You are my sunshine, my only sunshine."

JACK. I think you've had too much punch.

DOC. "I want to sit on your pulpit!"

JACK. You do?

DOC. You can't deny it. You feel just as I do! It was all there, in your letter.

JACK. My letter?

DOC. "Take me. Ravish me. Enter my house!"

JACK. Leo! Come out already! It's time to come out! ... Oh, no. The screen! There's nobody behind the screen!

DOC. Good idea. We can do it back there.

(He drags JACK behind the screen.)

JACK. No!

DOC. Please! Darling. Stephanie. I'm on my knees. *(He realizes he's not, so he drops to his knees and takes JACK's hand.)* Marry me.

(At this moment, BUTCH and AUDREY burst into the room having a fight.)

BUTCH. I can't believe you want to break up!

AUDREY. Butch I'm really sorry!

BUTCH. It's that Jack guy, isn't it? Oh, I'm gonna punch him—

AUDREY. Leave him alone!

BUTCH. I could have other girls, you know. Father wants me to marry Stephanie. And look at her! She's beautiful! Maybe I should marry her!

JACK. No, I really don't think — *(BUTCH kisses JACK.)* YAAAH!

DOC. Butch, listen to me. I know this may hurt you a little, but Stephanie and I are in love.

JACK. We are?

BUTCH. Father! You can't have her! She's mine now!

DOC. She wants me, Butch. Not you!

(And DOC kisses JACK.)

JACK. YAAAH! ... Would you two stop it!

(JACK runs around the room pursued by DOC, BUTCH and AUDREY.)

DOC. Stephanie, darling, come back!
BUTCH. Hey, leave her alone! She's mine!
AUDREY. Butch, wait! ... Butch!

(They all run out of the room. As soon as they're gone, LEO ENTERS as MAXINE — just as MEG ENTERS from the other direction. She's extremely upset.)

MEG. Oh, Maxine! Where have you been?! I need to talk to you!

LEO. My dear, what's the matter?

MEG. I need your advice! I don't know what to do!

LEO. Now, now, just calm down and start at the beginning. And whatever it is: Follow your heart. It's always the way.

MEG. All right. It's about Leo. You know how well I've gotten to know him over the past few weeks and oh, I just think the world of him. He's gentle, and thoughtful, and ...

LEO. Kind and handsome. Go on, go on.

MEG. Well, tonight, while I was dancing with him, he... kissed me. And when he did, something totally unexpected happened. Inside me. And I realized, while I was kissing him... oh, I don't know how to say this.

LEO. Try, try.

MEG. I'm sure it's wrong.

LEO. Tell me.

MEG. Oh, I can't do it!

LEO. Margaret, tell me right now.

MEG. ... All right. *(They sit together on the sofa.)* While I was kissing him, I was... thinking about you. *(She leans amorously into Maxine.)* Maxine, I think I'm in love with you.

(Pause.)

LEO. ... No. You're not.

MEG. I think I am.

LEO. You are not! Oh, darling, you're just confused. I mean, of course Leo and I are similar in some ways ...

MEG. Like two halves of the same apple! I mean, do I love him at all? Yes of course I do. He's funny and kind and ...

LEO. Sexy?

MEG. Well I guess a little bit. But the thing is, I love you more! I guess it's wrong, but it just feels, when you're not around me, that something is missing. I wouldn't have dared say anything, but I know you feel the same way. I know it. I can see it sometimes when you look at me. Sort of cross-eyed with your mouth hanging open.

LEO. No, that's just me.

MEG. Maxine, I'm being very brave and you aren't helping me!

LEO. I will help you, just listen! Life can be complicated. Right now it's extremely complicated. For reasons that have nothing to do with you.

MEG. You don't love me, do you?

LEO. Of course I love you —

MEG. But not the same way.

LEO. Well not exactly —

MEG. Oh, Maxine, I shouldn't have told you. I should just marry Duncan.

LEO. No, you shouldn't!

MEG. I'll never mention it again.

LEO. Mention it, please —

MEG. I am so sorry!

(She kisses MAXINE on the cheek and MEG runs up the stairs and into her room.)

LEO. No. Meg, wait —! Wait!

(She's gone. At which point, JACK ENTERS still dressed as Stephanie, but completely disheveled.)

JACK. Where the hell were you! You weren't there! Behind the screen! And I was attacked!

LEO. By Duncan?

JACK. No! By Doctor Lust, Monster of Medicine. He thought the letter was for him.

LEO. Why?

JACK. How should I know! Duncan must have thought I was insane.

LEO. Did he try anything?

JACK. No, he stuffed a telegram in my hand. Maybe, for a minister, that's foreplay.

LEO. What telegram? What did it say?

JACK. I don't know! I didn't read it!

LEO. Do you still have it?

JACK. I guess... Yes, here it is. So what?

LEO. "Apologize for delay. Stop."

JACK. "General strike at fault. Stop."

LEO. "Will arrive at eight fifteen tonight. Stop."

JACK. "Maxine and Stephanie."

LEO & JACK. ... YAHHHHH!

LEO. Eight fifteen! That's in five minutes! What do we do?!

JACK. Get the hell out of here!

LEO. But I can't leave Meg.

JACK. Forget about Meg! We're about to get arrested as women! They'd put us in a woman's prison. With female truck drivers with tight t-shirts and tattoos! ... Well, maybe that's not so bad...

LEO. Wait a second. If we're men, we're in the clear.

JACK. What do you mean?

LEO. When the girls arrive, everybody will be looking for the first Maxine and Stephanie. So we have to change and become Leo and Jack again!

JACK. Good idea.

DUNCAN. *(Off.)* Florence, just don't ask questions!

LEO & JACK. ... Duncan

(They hide under the stairs, as DUNCAN ENTERS at a run from the garden, pulling Florence along with him.)

DUNCAN. Oh, damn, I thought I saw them in here.

FLORENCE. Duncan, what are you doing?!

DUNCAN. All right, listen. The women you know as Maxine and Stephanie are frauds. The real ones are arriving tonight.

FLORENCE. How do you know?

DUNCAN. A telegram just arrived. And there was one before that.

FLORENCE. Let me see them.

DUNCAN. I don't have them right now.

FLORENCE. Oh, please —

DUNCAN. It's the truth!

(Bing bong! The front doorbell rings.)

DUNCAN. It's them. It has to be. Come on!

FLORENCE. Ah!

(DUNCAN pulls FLORENCE off at breakneck speed. As soon as DUNCAN and FLORENCE are gone, LEO and JACK come out of hiding. Simultaneously, MEG ENTERS from her bedroom, at the top of the stairs. She sees the men from above, but they don't see her.)

JACK. Oh, God in heaven. It's incredible! Just look at us! Two grown men dressed as women!

(Both men pull off their wigs. MEG reels backward against the wall, then clings onto the banister, peering down through the rails.)

JACK. I'm wearing a dress, for God's sake. And a petticoat! And lace knickers! With little flowers on them! I think they're peonies!

(AUDREY now ENTERS from down the hall. She starts to say something to MEG, but MEG silences her and points over the balcony to the men below.)

JACK. If my mother ever saw me like this, I'd kill myself!

(AUDREY takes it in — and swoons into MEG's arms. MEG pushes her back to her feet.)

JACK. Oh, how did I ever let you talk me into this?
LEO. You weren't complaining for the last four weeks, while you were slobbering over Audrey.
JACK. Well what about you? If I hadn't gone along with all this, you wouldn't have met Meg.

LEADING LADIES

LEO. Well that's true. Except now she says she's attracted to Maxine.

JACK. Attracted?

LEO. Attracted.

(AUDREY turns and looks at Meg... then inches away from her.)

JACK. But you're not even pretty as a girl.

LEO. Look who's talking!

JACK. Well, I can't be too bad, because two men just kissed me on the lips!

(The women react.)

LEO. Look, that's not the point! The point is, I'm in love with Meg. She is the greatest woman that ever walked this earth. I don't care if she's slow, I don't care if she's gullible, I don't even mind that squint she has in the one eye. I'm in love with her.

JACK. Gee, that's really nice, it's a lovely thought, I know just how you feel BUT I NEED MY CLOTHES!

LEO. All right, all right! Come on. We'll both change, then find the girls and tell them everything. But we have to do it just right, because this whole thing makes them look really, really stupid.

(The men EXIT and the women head down the stairs.)

MEG. *(Beyond furious — ready to eat nails.)* I'll kill him. I'm going to kill him!

AUDREY. I think we should kill all four of them! ... Oh. I get it, I get it.

MEG. Unh!

AUDREY. But, you know, when I think about all they've been going through just to spend a little time with us, I'm incredulous. That means —

MEG. Shut up!

AUDREY. Yeah! I'm gonna shut up now!

MEG. I can't believe I shared a bedroom with him for four weeks! *(A horrible thought suddenly strikes her.)* Oh my God. He saw me in my... curlers! *(She's seething now.)* Revenge. I want revenge!

(MEG EXITS in a fury into the garden.)

AUDREY. *(Calling.)* Yeah! Me, too!

(At which moment, JACK hurries in from the kitchen, dressed as himself.)

JACK. Audrey!

AUDREY. Jack!

JACK. Listen. There's something I have to tell you.

AUDREY. Well, I have something to — !

JACK. Please don't interrupt. *(He takes a breath and it all pours out.)* I did something terrible. It all started a month ago. Leo and I were on a train.

(AUDREY reacts as if to say "no kidding".)

JACK. Well you know that. And we read about Florence dying and leaving her money to Max and Steve. And by this time I had met you and all I wanted to do was take you in my arms. But then you told us her nephews were Maxine and Stephanie, and you see we're actors and we had these costumes and so... well the fact is, we dressed up as women!

AUDREY. No!

JACK. Yes! I was that beautiful creature. Stephanie. It was me.

AUDREY. Wow!

JACK. I know, but I didn't mean to make you look stupid. I— I did it because of your thighs. I mean your eyes. I wanted to be with every inch of you. Your lips. Your forehead. And I wanted your bust. I mean your trust. And I want a home so badly. A real home with a picket fence, and a gate, and little Audreys skating to school every morning. And so I lay my soul at your feet and I ask — nay, I beg — your forgiveness. *(He kneels before her.)* Audrey, will you marry me?

AUDREY. You are the most obstreperous, abominable, loathsome, odious, deplorable, despicable, obnoxious, vile, detestable man I have ever met! And of course I'll marry you! You just had to ask! Now give us a hug!

(She grabs him, they hug and run off. The moment they're gone, LEO and MEG ENTER from opposite directions. LEO is now in his suit, as LEO. MEG plays it cool, enjoying her revenge to the hilt.)

LEO. Meg!

MEG. Leo, listen to me, I have to talk to you!

LEO. Well I have something to tell you too.

MEG. Let me go first, it's important. After I left you on the dance floor, I went to see Maxine. I was confused, and oh, I said some silly things, but while I was with her, she gave me some very good advice. She told me that I should follow my heart. And now that I've had a chance to think, I know exactly what she meant. So I'm marrying Duncan tomorrow morning.

LEO. Huh?

MEG. "Follow your heart." I made a commitment to him. That's what she meant. She wants me to marry him.

LEO. No, she doesn't.

MEG. That was her way of reminding me that honor and trust are so important!

LEO. No they're not! That's not what she meant!

MEG. Leo. Thank you for everything. Good-bye.

(She kisses him sadly on the cheek and starts to go. She has to do this, but now it's breaking her heart.)

LEO. No! Wait! Look, look, look! Wait, wait! Look! Wait! Look! I'll go find Maxine and she'll tell you exactly what she thinks.

MEG. I know what she thinks.

LEO. No you don't! I mean, you-you-you think you know ...

MEG. I'm sorry, Leo.

LEO. Please. Please! Just one more chance! Let her talk to you! Please!

MEG. ... All right. I'll give her one minute to come in here and tell me what she thinks. And if she isn't here by then I'm marrying Duncan. Oh, and I want you to be here too. You and Maxine together. Then we'll get it all straightened out.

LEO. Together?

MEG. That's right.

LEO. Together! Right! One minute! Me and Leo. Me and Maxine! I'll find her. And mail her. Bring her. We'll be here! *(He dashes off through the garden. Off:)* Shit!

(At that moment, DUNCAN and FLORENCE ENTER from the hall.)

DUNCAN. Margaret! We've been looking all over for you. I'm afraid I have some rather distressing news.

LEADING LADIES

FLORENCE. Don't listen to him! He's an idiot.

DUNCAN. Florence, please. Margaret, I now have conclusive proof that the two women who have been here for the past four weeks posing as Maxine and Stephanie are not your cousins.

MEG. *(Sadly.)* I know that, Duncan.

DUNCAN. You do? How?

MEG. It doesn't matter.

DUNCAN. Oh. Well, I do have some good news. Your real cousins have just arrived. They're in the garden.

FLORENCE. And I don't particularly like them!

DUNCAN. That's not the point! And Meg, listen, I've spoken to them and they're willing to take only $100,000 each and go back to England. We'll have the rest for the Foundation! Now as soon as the police arrive, this will all be over.

MEG. *(Alarmed.)* The police? What for?

DUNCAN. To arrest Maxine and Stephanie. That is, the supposed ones.

FLORENCE. I told him not to do it!

DUNCAN. Florence, they have deceived you.

FLORENCE. But I like them, Duncan!

DUNCAN. Well I'm sorry, but they have broken the law! They have made a mockery of your entire household and they should not be rewarded for their... theatrical behavior. So typical of actors, it's always me, me, me, look at me!

(At this moment, we hear the whine of a siren as a police car screeches to a halt in the driveway.)

DUNCAN. Oh, good! Now all I have to do is find them and hand them over.

MEG. Duncan! Wait! I saw one of them in the front yard! Just now!

DUNCAN. Which one?!
MEG. Stephanie. And Maxine. They were both there.
DUNCAN. I'll be right back!

(He runs off. The moment he's gone, LEO hurries in dressed as MAXINE, but slightly askew, since everything has been pulled on in such a hurry.)

LEO. Darling girl, there you are! Now listen, you misunderstood me. I want you to marry Leo, that divine young man — and he's right outside. *(Calling.)* Come in, darling! ... What?! What's that you said?! *(To MEG.)* Oh no! He's hurt his leg! I'll send him in. You stay right here.
MEG. Leo —

(He runs off and now plays both parts, putting his head around the door as necessary.)

LEO. *(Off — as LEO.)* Meg, I'm right out here! I've hurt my leg and I can't come in! *(Off — as MAXINE.)* Of course you can, just put a little weight on it. *(Off — as LEO.)* Ow, that really hurts!

(He pops his head around the door, without the wig and with his jacket on, as LEO. The more he can pop in and out as the two characters and make this a tour de force, as in "The Mystery of Irma Vep" and other similar plays, the better. It should build to a fever pitch.)

LEO. *(As LEO.)* Here I am, Meg! Now Maxine says you should marry me — but I've hurt my leg so I'll let her do all the talking. Bye!
MEG. Leo —

LEADING LADIES

LEO. *(Off — as Maxine.)* Oh you brave young man! Of course she should marry you and not Duncan! *(Off — as LEO.)* Then go inside and tell her! *(Off — as MAXINE.)* I'll do it right now!

MEG. Leo — !

(He runs back on as Maxine.)

LEO. I'm right here! Here I am! Now Meg, you really must marry Leo. He's such a lovely boy, and so handsome and —

MEG. Leo, stop it!

LEO. Leo? *(Beat; then he calls through the door:)* Leo, she's talking to you so listen carefully!

MEG. Would you please just stop it! I know it's you! I know you're Leo! And that Stephanie is Jack! I know everything!

LEO. You do?

MEG. Yes! Now get out of here, fast. The police are here!

LEO. But I can't leave you.

MEG. You have to! You'll be arrested!

LEO. Meg, I love you.

MEG. I know that! And I love you!

LEO. You do?

MEG. Yes.

LEO. Will you marry me?

MEG. Yes!

(He's about to kiss her, but stops abruptly.)

LEO. Wait! I came here to take your money.

MEG. I know that!

(They kiss. Another really great kiss.)

FLORENCE. If I were you, I'd get the hell out of here.

LEO. *(To FLORENCE.)* Aren't you even a little surprised?

FLORENCE. Why? Because I'm old? Now listen carefully. Old: smart. Young: nitwits. Now go!

LEO. Right.

(LEO pulls his wig on and rushes to the garden doors — and runs straight into DUNCAN.)

DUNCAN. Aha! Gotcha!

MEG. Oh, no.

(Beat — then LEO transforms himself right back into MAXINE.)

LEO. Duncan. My dear old friend. How delightful to see you again. "Ah, the friends thou hast, grapple them to thy soul with hoops of steel."

DUNCAN. How very apt. Because you're under arrest.

(JACK ENTERS.)

JACK. Hey. What's going on?

MEG. Duncan, let her go!

DUNCAN. I will not! She's a fraud!

MEG. But wait a second! What if she's the real one and the ones outside aren't genuine?

DUNCAN. Margaret, please. You admitted she was a fraud, not five minutes ago. You may like this creature, but your real cousins are in the garden waiting for you!

(From the garden, we hear voices and gunshots.)

LEADING LADIES

A WOMAN'S VOICE. *(Off.)* AHHHHHHHHH! *(They all look up.)* Leave me alone! Get your hands off me! Stop it!

(BANG!)

A SECOND WOMAN'S VOICE. *(Off.)* Get away from me! Do you hear me?!

(BANG! BANG!)

MEN'S and WOMEN'S VOICES. *(Off.)* Grab 'em! Hold 'em! Ahhhh! I got 'em! Ahhhhhh!

(BANG! BANG!)

A MAN'S VOICE. *(Off.)* Quiet down! You're under arrest!

(AUDREY rushes in from the garden, with BUTCH and DOC trailing behind. They're crazed with excitement.)

AUDREY. Oh my gosh! The most incredible thing just happened! I'm out there talking to these two women, and they tell me their names are Maxine and Stephanie. And my jaw, it hits the floor, ya know?! Then out of the blue two policemen show up and then whamo! They take one look at these women and go "Aha! Trixie McCall! Bubbles Schaeffer! Hands up!" Then the girls make a run for it, and the policemen knock 'em down! It turns out the girls are well-known crooks! They sent a telegram and pretended to be your nieces just to get your money! Can you imagine?!

LEO. Oh, this wicked, wicked world.

DUNCAN. Oh, no.

MEG. Duncan. I believe you owe "Maxine" an apology.

LEO. No, no, please. Don't. We all make mistakes. It is forgiveness that makes the world a better place. Reverend Wooley got a little confused, and don't we all sometimes?

MEG. Yes, we do.

AUDREY. Yeah. Tell me about it. Hey Jack.

(She kisses JACK on the lips. A great kiss.)

DUNCAN. Audrey!

LEO. Now it's our turn.

(MAXINE kisses MEG.)

DUNCAN. Margaret!!!

MEG. Oh, stop it. We should tell him the truth.

DUNCAN. Tell me what?!

LEO. *(As MAXINE.)* Margaret and I are getting married.

DUNCAN. AHHHHHHHHHHHHHHHH!

DOC. Don't you get any ideas, Florence. You're too old for me. *(There's no answer. They all look at FLORENCE. She's slumped over in her chair.)* Florence ...? Florence! *(Everyone freezes. DOC tries to get a pulse at her neck, but there is none. He feels her hands. They're stone cold. DOC goes white.)* She's gone.

MEG. Oh, no ...

AUDREY. Florence ...

(Everyone is in shock. MEG takes LEO's hand. DOC shakes his head sadly.)

FLORENCE. ... You are the worst doctor that ever lived.

(Shock, then cries of relief, as everyone clusters around her,

LEADING LADIES

jubilant.)

MEG/AUDREY/BUTCH/JACK. Aunt Florence!/You're alive!/ You really had us scared that time/Oh, Lord ...

(A bell sounds.)

AUDREY. Oh my gosh. It's time for the show!
LEO. Places, everyone! Act One places! Let's go!

(Everyone scurries around to prepare for the play, moving furniture and pulling a costume basket in from the kitchen. During the following, the actors pull costume pieces from the basket and put them on.)

EVERYONE. The chair! Put it here!/ We need the hats!/I've got mine./What about the wig?/Where's my sword! I need my sword!/ My line! I can't remember my first line!

(Meanwhile, LEO and MEG have a moment alone together, and we hear them over the words above.)

LEO. What did you mean that "maybe" I was a little sexy?
MEG. I was just teasing. Because I knew it was you all along.
LEO. You did not!
MEG. I did so! From the moment you walked through the door, I knew there was something funny going on because

(He stops her mouth with a kiss.)

JACK. Would you two stop it! We have a show to put on!
LEO. I'm ready!

MEG. Me too!
DOC. Ready!
BUTCH. Ready!
JACK. Ready!
FLORENCE. Ready!
DUNCAN. Ready.
AUDREY. All set!
LEO. Ladies and gentlemen, the curtain is going up,
EVERYONE. AND THE PLAY BEGINS!

(Blackout.)

CURTAIN

LEADING LADIES

CURTAIN CALL - NOTE

As some readers may know, my play *Lend Me A Tenor* has a rather unique curtain call built into the script. I first thought of it during rehearsals for the first big commercial production of the play that was produced by Andrew Lloyd Webber in London. At the conclusion of the play proper, the cast reenacts the entire play at top speed, in about 85 seconds, to a wild piece of music by Jacques Ibert. Since the night we first tried it in London, this curtain call has always had a wonderfully enthusiastic response from the audience.

After I wrote *Leading Ladies*, I wanted to come up with something similarly fun and exuberant – but slightly different – for the end of the piece; but try as I might, I couldn't come up with one. If you turn to page 107 of this book and read "Curtain Call – Option 2," you'll see what I did come up with when I directed the first production of the play at the Alley Theatre in Houston: some good suggestions, but nothing concrete.

Then in January 2007, I got a call from a wonderful director named Brad Carroll. Brad (who is also a terrific composer) had just directed *Leading Ladies* in Phoenix and called me to say that he and a colleague, Adrian Balbontin, had come up with an idea for the curtain call and what did I think of it.

Well, I think it's terrific, and I reprint it here with their permission. Essentially, it's a speeded up version of the play to another wild piece of music (Leroy Anderson's "Fiddle Faddle"), but it tells the story of the play backwards. And the clever thing is that this makes sense, since the last line of the play is "AND THE PLAY BEGINS!"

So I recommend using this curtain call to everyone producing the play, and I thank Brad and Adrian for being so ingenious – and for being so generous in sharing it with all of us.

Two notes: First, remember that the idea of this curtain call is to reenact the story of the play (backwards): so the trick is to run to each "pose" and

LEADING LADIES

hold it long enough so that the audience knows where it is. As in the case of the curtain call for *Lend Me A Tenor*, there are no spoken lines.

Second, I strongly suspect that this curtain call, like the one in *Tenor*, will end up feeling, in the end, like a part of the play as a whole and that, because of the music and laughter it provokes, it will not allow the audience to really applaud for the cast. So I recommend that you provide a traditional "curtain call" after this faux call. And then everyone will go home happy.

I hope you enjoy every second of the play – and the curtain call!

-Ken Ludwig

LEADING LADIES

CURTAIN CALL - Option 1

Created by Brad Carroll and Adrian Balbontin
(performed to Leroy Anderson's "Fiddle Faddle")
Remember: there are no spoken lines.
The lines written below are only to remind you where we are.

BLACKOUT. Music begins. Lights up.

1. Final tableau
   ALL move to:

2. Dead Florence in the chair
   Duncan enter SL doors
   ALL move to:

3. Duncan "AHHHHHH!" (After "Margaret and I are getting married")
   ALL move to:

4. Audrey "oh my gosh" speech (about Trixie and Bubbles)
   Audrey/Butch/Doc exit garden; Jack exit UC
   Others move to:

5. Duncan/Leo "Aha! Gotcha!" at garden doors
   Duncan/Leo exit garden
   Meg/Flo move to:

6. Leo/Maxine quick change at garden doors biz
   (Leo do quick "shuffle off to Buffalo" step - wig on/off/on/off
   then "oh, forget it" gesture to audience, then exit garden doors)
   Flo exit UC; Meg exit UC
   Audrey/Jack enter SL doors for:

7. Jack propose to Audrey pose
   Audrey x to upstairs landing;
   Meg enter from bedroom to join Audrey
   Jack x to UC; Leo enter from garden, join Jack UC for:

8. Leo/Jack "look at us, grown men dressed as women" reveal
   (Meg and Audrey aghast above)
   A exit upstairs hallway; J exit UC

M x downstairs to join Leo; Leo x and sit on couch for:

9. Meg/Maxine "life can be complicated" Maxine fall off couch
    Meg chase Maxine off to garden
    Doc/Stephanie (Jack)/Butch/Audrey chase on from UC for:

10. Doc kiss Jack (Stephanie), Butch kiss Jack,
    Jack look to audience "Ahhhhh!"
    Audrey/Butch exit garden; Jack/Doc x to couch for:

11. Doc/Jack (Stephanie) seduction pose on couch
    Doc exit UC; Jack x to landing above;
    Duncan enter SL doors, x DR for:

12. Jack/Duncan – Stephanie's "Hello big boy!"
    Jack exit into bedroom; Duncan exit to garden;
    Doc (w/letter) enter UC, drop to knees at C for:

13. Doc w/letter "God in heaven!"
    Doc exit UC;
    Meg enter upper hallway; Leo enter SL doors
    Meg x downstairs and join Leo for:

14. Meg/Leo "Fred and Ginger" moment
    (meet DL- dance out into garden)
    Audrey/Butch enter UC; Doc/Jack enter SL doors;
    Duncan/Flo enter SR doors, all 6 meet DC for:

15. TANGO final pose
    Audrey/Butch/Doc/Jack exit UC
    Duncan x to phone; Flo x to garden doors for:

16. Duncan on phone/Flo's Tango entrance pose in doorway
    Duncan exit SL; Flo exit garden;
    Audrey/Butch/Doc/Jack/Meg enter UC;
    Leo enter SR doors for:

17. End of rehearsal scene (Quintet)
    (Doc step down, do "rollicking"; Butch step down, do
    "Mississippi"; Jack step down, do "Olivia" pose; Meg step

down, do "manly Cesario" pose; Audrey step down, do "Bran
do" pose)

Butch/Doc exit SR doors; Leo exit garden; Audrey exit UC
Duncan enter SL doors (with telegram) hold on landing;
Meg stay C for:

18. Meg banish Duncan - " now go, I have to study my lines"
    Duncan x DR; Meg start SL then follow Duncan DR for:

19. Meg/Duncan telegram moment
    Duncan x out UC; Meg x to mirror;
    Leo enter garden, pose DR for:

20. Meg shimmy at mirror, turn and see Leo DR, "eeek!"
    Leo exit garden; Meg exit upstairs bedroom;
    Duncan enter UC, x to phone for:

21. Duncan on phone, hear Meg offstage
    Jack enter from upstairs bedroom, x downstairs to SL landing
    Meg enter from bedroom; Audrey enter from upstairs hallway;
    Leo enter from garden for:

22. MIRACLE pose (end of Act 1) (complete with light cue)
    Jack exit SL doors; A off hallway
    Leo x DR (jump up and down while waiting for Meg)
    Meg x downstairs to join Leo (jumping up and down) DR for:

23. Meg/Maxine "Eeeeeee!" moment
    Flo enter SR; Duncan enter SL doors;
    Audrey enter UC; Butch/Doc enter SR doors;
    Leo x to garden doors landing;
    J enter UC, join Leo on landing for:

24. Flo heart attack moment
    Jack/Leo x to behind couch; Flo x to UC;
    others adjust to position for:

25. Flo "they're so beautiful" presentation moment
    Flo exit SR; Jack/Leo x DC; others adjust for:

LEADING LADIES

26. Maxine/Steph "Auntie Florence is dead" crying moment
    CURTAIN IN
    Others disperse as curtain falls
    Meg/Duncan x DR/DL for:

27. Meg/Duncan telephone scene pose
    Meg/Duncan exit SR/SL
    Jack/Leo enter C curtain (Leo w/newspaper) for:

28. TRAIN – double time sign language moment
    Both x DC for:

29. Leo/Jack – "we could be brothers" take to audience pose
    Jack exit C curtain
    Leo stay for:

30. Leo – newspaper "idea" take
    Jack re-enter w/swords, hand one to Leo for:

31. Leo/Jack sword fight (3 moments from fight, in reverse order)
    Jack/Leo exit SL/SR
    Doc enter C curtain for:

32. Doc – "Awhoo! Thank You!!" moment
    Doc exit SL
    CURTAIN OUT to reveal:

33. Duncan on phone "is that Grandma Kunkle?"/Meg collapse on couch
    Duncan exit SL doors
    Meg x upstairs for:

34. Entrance pose on landing above, then exit bedroom door, hold, slam
    door on button of music!

BLACKOUT

Note: In the Curtain Call Jack is dressed as Jack and Leo is dressed as Maxine (as they were when the curtain fell).

CURTAIN CALL - Option 2

The Curtain Call is accompanied by Leonard Bernstein's Overture to Candide.*

Every effort should be made to make the Curtain Call into some form of the Twelfth Night performance that we've been anticipating. One possibility *(Which was used in the first production)* is that, as the Curtain Call starts, a large flip-board is brought in. The first card read:

THE FLORENCE SNIDER PLAYERS
PRESENT
TWELFTH NIGHT!

Then, as each character comes on for his or her bow, a new card appears with the Twelfth Night character name of that actor. Each actor wears some part of his or her Twelfth Night costume, poses and bows. The cards read:

SIR ANDREW AGUECHEEK
SIR TOBY BELCH
SEBASTIAN, A GUY
MALVOLIO, THE STEWARD
FESTE, THE JESTER
THE COUNTESS OLIVIA
THE DUKE ORSINO
VIOLA, OUR HEROINE

---

*Permission to use the overture recording of "Candide" for this purpose must be obtained by Sony/BMG Music Entertainment, www.sonybmg.com.

Alternatively — and better yet — the Curtain Call could consist of the cast putting on Twelfth Night in an abbreviated, two-minute form, the zanier the better. HOWEVER: I tried doing it this way in the world premiere production, and it didn't quite work because the spoken lines of Twelfth Night stopped people clapping — and the audience became confused, wondering if they were watching a curtain call or an additional part of the play. So perhaps Twelfth Night can be indicated in some way without words but only music.

In any case, here's the text I wrote *(and used once)* for the spoken curtain call. Perhaps a director who is a lot smarter than I am can use it as the basis for something great:

(A large banner drops down saying: "CURTAIN CALL! TWELFTH NIGHT!" Then another banner drops down saying "SCENE ONE: A SEACOAST AFTER A SHIPWRECK.")

VIOLA/MEG. Captain! What country, friend, is this?
CAPTAIN/DOC. *(With only one leg, a crutch and an eye patch.)* This is Illyria, lady. Home of the Duke Orsino!
VIOLA/MEG. I'll serve this Duke, dressed not as a maid, but as a man.
CAPTAIN/DOC. A man?! Haw, haw! A man! Shiver me timbers!

(He stumps off. More running around as another banner drops into place: "SCENE TWO: THE DUKE'S HOUSE.")

ORSINO/LEO. If music be the food of love, play on! *(VIOLA runs on dressed as a man.)* Young man, fair youth, get thee to the Countess Olivia, And there unfold the passion of my love.

VIOLA/MEG. I shall, my lord. *(Aside.)*Yet a barful strife,
Who'ere I woo myself would be his wife!

(More running around, then another banner: "SCENE THREE: THE GARDEN." Sir Toby and Sir Andrew enter.)

SIR TOBY/DOC. Ha! Ha! Ho! Ho! Ha! Ha! Rollicking.
SIR ANDREW/BUTCH. Sir Toby Belch, your-niece-Olivia-will-not-be-seen! *(Mississippi.)* Or if she be it's four to one she'll none of me! *(Mississippi!)*

(Running. Banner: "SCENE FOUR: OLIVIA'S MANSION.")

MARIA/FLORENCE. Milady, a young man is at the gate
                   Who represents the Duke Orsino and
                   would
                   Press his suit.
                   (She thinks about "press his suit.")

OLIVIA/JACK. Let him approach.

(VIOLA ENTERS.)

VIOLA/MEG. Most radiant, exquisite and unmatchable beauty,
My lord and master loves you!
OLIVIA/JACK. *(Aside.)* How now?!
                   Methinks I feel this youth's perfections
                   With an invisible and subtle stealth
                   To creep in at mine eyes.
VIOLA/MEG. Madam?
OLIVIA/JACK. Get you to your lord.
                   I cannot love him. Let him send no more,

> Unless, perchance, you come to me again
> To tell me how he takes it.

VIOLA/MEG. Egad! She loves me sure!
>   Disguise, I see thou art a wickedness
>   Wherein the pregnant enemy does much.

(Running. Banner: "SCENE FIVE: A STREET.")

SEBASTIAN/AUDREY. *(Dressed identically to VIOLA, she ENTERS from the opposite direction from which VIOLA just exited, while OLIVIA hasn't moved. Imitating Brando —)* Ah, me. My stars shine darkly over me. I seek in this strange land my twin sister.

OLIVIA/JACK. *(Seeing Sebastian.)* Ah! Back so soon?! Mwa! Oh handsome youth, woulds't thou be ruled by me?

SEBASTIAN/AUDREY. *(Brando.)* I would.

(Running. Banner: "SCENE SIX: THE GARDEN AGAIN.")

MALVOLIO/DUNCAN. *(Dressed in yellow stockings, cross-gartered with a page-boy wig; he's not happy.)* Wilt thou have me, lady? Malvolio? Thy steward?

OLIVIA/JACK. Sir, I cannot. Are you mad?

MALVOLIO/DUNCAN. Some are born great, some achieve greatness, and some have greatness thrust upon them.

(Running. Banner: "GRAND FINALÉ!")

ORSINO/LEO. Come away, good youth. Olivia has no eyes for me.

OLIVIA/JACK. *(To Viola.)* Wait! Caesario, husband, stay!
ORSINO/LEO. "Husband?!"
VIOLA/MEG. What?!

LEADING LADIES

ORSINO/LEO. O thou dissembling cub!
VIOLA/MEG. My lord, I do protest! I did not marry her!
SEBASTIAN/AUDREY. *(Leaping in to the rescue.)* He's right!
Twas I, Sebastian!

(VIOLA and SEBASTIAN are wearing the exact same outfit, and everyone gasps audibly at the resemblance.)

ORSINO/LEO. An apple cleft in two is not more twin
Than these two creatures!
OLIVIA/JACK. Twins!
SIR TOBY/DOC. Identical!
SEBASTIAN/AUDREY. Sister!
VIOLA/MEG. Brother!
OLIVIA/JACK. Husband!
SEBASTIAN/AUDREY. Wife!
ORSINO/LEO. Wife!
VIOLA/MEG. Husband!
MARIA/FLORENCE. Mistress!
SIR ANDREW/BUTCH. Steward!
MALVOLIO/DUNCAN. Fool!
SIR TOBY/DOC. Ha ha!
EVERYONE. Curtain!

(Blackout.)

LEADING LADIES

PROP & SET DRESSING

FURNITURE
Sofa
4 chairs
Sofa Table
Screen
Bookcase
Lawn furniture
Rug
Train Seats
Buffet
Armchair
Small table
2 wooden step ladders

SET DRESSING
Foliage
Pot/runs
Painting
Painting on wall in upstage room
Painting offstage left
Set of 3 small prints on wall
Wall Mirror
Throw Pillows
Lightswitch
Cushions for patio furniture
Books
Framed photos
Vases
Dishes/pitcher & basin
Umbrella stand

LEADING LADIES

ACT I
Purse
Skull
Roller Skates
Text Books
Newspaper
Hold-All
Towel
Telegram
Suitcases
Newspaper?
Costumes
Wigs (in suitcase)
Flowers
Towel
"Welcome Home" banner - hung onstage (using 2 wooden step ladders)

ACT II
Telephone
Several purchases including a dress box
Telegram
Sword
Baldric or sword belt
Battered Sword
Baldric or sword belt
Script
Carpet Bag
Letter in an envelope
Hankie
Letter in an envelope
Telegram #2

LEADING LADIES

Carpet Bag
Floral arrangement
Standing floral arrangements

LEADING LADIES

COSTUMES
Run Schedule

TOP OF SHOW

Character	Location / Action	Costume Piece	Where
MEG	Preset	White Hat	onstage - on DSL chair
MEG	Preset	White Gloves	onstage - on DSL chair
MEG	Preset	Blue clutch	onstage - on DSL chair
MEG	Preset	Stole	onstage - on DSL chair
LEO/Maxine	Preset	Shoes, Pants,	
LEO/Maxine	Preset	Cleopatra costume	USR
JACK/Stephanie	Preset	Titania Costume	USR
JACK/Stephanie	Preset	Beard and costumes in carpet bag	DSR
LEO/Maxine	Preset	Jacket on train seat	SL set of seats, Onstage seat
JACK/Stephanie	Preset	Jacket on train seat	SR set of seats, Offstage seat

END OF ACT 1, SCENE 1

Character	Location / Action	Change From	Change To
MEG	DSR	Polka dot dress	Skirt & twin set

INTERNAL ACT 1, SCENE 2

Character	Location / Action	Costume Piece	Where
LEO/Maxine	Move	Pants, shoes	UCL

END OF ACT 1 SCENE 2 into ACT 1 SCENE 3

Character	Location / Action	Change From	Change To
LEO	UC (L)	Hamlet	Suit, Loose tunic, shoes; ADD: pants, shoes, (Jacket set on train seat)
JACK	UC (R)	Polonious	Suit underdressed, Robe off, hat off; Jacket on train seat
DOC	Back of House	Lodge member	DOC
BUTCH	Back of House	Lodge member	BUTCH

LEADING LADIES

INTERNAL ACT 1, SCENE 3

Character	Location / Action	Change From	Change To
AUDREY		Shoes	Roller skates

END OF ACT 1, SCENE 5

Character	Location / Action	Change From	Change To
AUDREY	UC	Roller Skates	Shoes
LEO	UC	Suit	Leo as Cleopatra
JACK	UC	Suit	JACK as Titania

INTERNAL ACT 1, SCENE 6

Character	Location / Action	Change From	Change To
BUTCH	SR	BUTCH	Sir Andrew Costume
FLORENCE	SR	PJ's and slippers	PJ's #2 and slippers
DOC	SR	DOC	Toby Costume
MEG	UC-2nd floor	Skirt & Twin set	Towel

END OF ACT 1, SCENE 6 into ACT 2, SCENE 1

Character	Location / Action	Change From	Change To
JACK/Stephanie	UR	Titania	Stephanie Day Dress
LEO/Maxine		Cleopatra	LEO repeat pants of 1.3
MEG		Towel	Coat/Hat/Dress and purse
AUDREY		Tastee Bite Uniform	Sebastian costume
LEO/Maxine	Preset	Maxine Jumpsuit, shoes, sunglasses, scarf Look 6	
JACK/Stephanie	Preset	Stephanie "in Robe"	
JACK/Stephanie	Preset	JACK look 6 (pants, polo shirt, and shoes)	
JACK/Stephanie	Preset	Olivia	
MEG	Preset	Cesario Costume	
LEO/Maxine	Preset	Maxine's Party Dress	
JACK/Stephanie	Preset	Stephanie's Party Dress	
MEG	Preset	Meg's Party Dress	
AUDREY	Preset	Audrey's Party Dress	
BUTCH	Preset	Rented Tux	
DOC	Preset	Rented Tux	

INTERNAL ACT 2, SCENE 1

Character	Location / Action	Change From	Change To
FLORENCE	SR	Pj bottoms and Robe	Party Dress

END OF ACT 2, SCENE 1 into ACT 2, SCENE 2

Character	Location / Action	Change From	Change To
JACK/Stephanie	UC	Stephanie Day Dress	Stephanie in Robe
MEG		Coat/Hat/Dress	Cesario Costume
DUNCAN		Preacher	Party Tux
MEG	STRIKE	Meg's Hat, Hat pin, Purse, and coat	

INTERNAL ACT 2, SCENE 2

Character	Location / Action	Change From	Change To
JACK/Stephanie	SL	Stephanie in Robe	JACK
LEO/Maxine	USR	Leo	Leo as Maxine in pants
JACK/Stephanie	SL	JACK	Olivia Costume

END OF ACT 2 SCENE 2 into ACT 2 SCENE 3

Character	Location / Action	Change From	Change To
LEO/Maxine	SL	Maxine in pants	Maxine Party Dress
JACK/Stephanie	SR	Olivia Costume	Stephanie Party Dress
MEG	SL	Cesario Costume	Party Dress
AUDREY	UC	Sebustian Costume	Party Dress
BUTCH	UR	Sir Andrew Costume	Rented Tux
DOC	SR	Toby Costume	Rented Tux

INTERNAL ACT 2, SCENE 3

Character	Location / Action	Change From	Change To
AUDREY	SR		ADD: Apron
AUDREY	SR		REMOVE: Apron
LEO/Maxine	USR	Leo dinner Jacket	Maxine Party Dress
JACK/Stephanie	SR		"Disheveled"
LEO/Maxine	MOVES	Leo's Tux	
LEO/Maxine	ENTERS	Carpet bag "w/LEO TUX"	
JACK/Stephanie	UC-2nd Floor	Stephanie Party Dress	JACK Dinner Jacket
LEO/Maxine	UC-2nd Floor	Maxine Party Dress	Leo Dinner Jacket

LEADING LADIES

LEO/Maxine	SL	Leo dinner Jacket	Maxine Party Dress
LEO/Maxine	SL	Maxine Party Dress	Leo's Head and Shoulder
LEO/Maxine	SL	Leo's Head and Shoulder	Maxine's Arm
LEO/Maxine	SL	Leo's Head	Maxine's Head

12th NIGHT PLAY   -   Curtain Call

Character	Location / Action	Costume Piece
DOC and BUTCH	Get	Large basket with Shakespeare costume pieces and props inside
DOC	ADDS	Captain hat and eye patch-under a big hat w/feather.
AUDREY	ADDS	Hat, shoes, and ruff
LEO/Maxine	SL	Maxine Party Dress
MEG	ADDS	Shawl and Hat
FLORENCE	ADDS	Apron
BUTCH	ADDS	Hat
JACK	ADDS	Olivia Hat and Handkerchief
FLORENCE	ADDS	ruff
DUNCAN	ADDS/ REMOVES	ADD: Ruff, Doublet/REMOVE: Pants (Underdressed w/Cross gartered Tights)
DOC	REMOVES/ADDS	REMOVES: Hat and Patch/ADDS: Cape and Hat w/feather

SET DESIGN
by Neil Patel

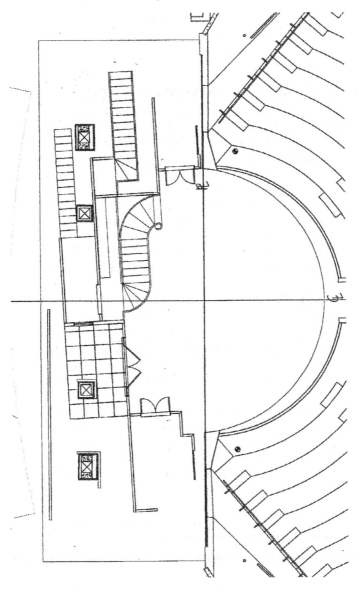

GREAT NEW COMEDIES BY KEN LUDWIG!!

SHAKESPEARE IN HOLLYWOOD

Lights, Camera, Shakespeare! It's 1934, and Shakespeare's most famous fairies, Oberon and Puck, have magically materialized on the Warner Bros. Hollywood set of Max Reinhardt's A Midsummer Night's Dream. Instantly smitten by the glitz and glamour of show biz, the two are ushered onto the silver screen to play (who else?) themselves. With a little help from a feisty flower, blonde bombshells, movie moguls, and arrogant "asses" are tossed into loopy love triangles, with raucous results. The mischievous magic of moviedom sparkles in this hilarious comic romp. WINNER of the 2004 Helen Hayes Award for Best New Play. 8m, 4f (20891)

BE MY BABY

The play tells the story of an irascible Scotsman and an uptight English woman who are unexpectedly thrown together on the journey of a lifetime. John and Maude are brought together when his ward marries her niece. Then, when the young couple decides to adopt a new born baby, the older couple has to travel 6,000 miles to California to pick up the child and bring her safely home to Scotland. The problem is, John and Maude despise each other. To make matters worse, they get stranded in San Francisco for several weeks and are expected to jointly care for the helpless newborn. There they form a new partnership and learn some startling lessons about life and love. 3m, 3f (#04879)

See the Samuel French website at **samuelfrench.com** or our **Basic Catalogue of Plays and Musicals** for more information.